THE SPY PARAMOUNT

E. PHILLIPS OPPENHEIM

THE BRITISH LIBRARY

This edition published in 2014 by

The British Library
96 Euston Road
London NW1 2DB

Originally published in London in 1935 by Hodder & Stoughton

© 2014 The Oppenheim–John Downes Memorial Trust

Cataloguing in Publication Data
A catalogue record for this book is available from The British Library

ISBN 978 0 7123 5767 8

Typeset by IDSUK (DataConnection) Ltd
Printed and bound in England by TJ International

The Oppenheim–John Downes Memorial Trust is a charitable body
established by E. Phillips Oppenheim's daughter, Mrs Elsie Downes,
to support British writers, painters, musicians and artists of every
description who are unable to pursue their vocation by
reason of financial need.

CONTENTS

		PAGE
CHAPTER	I	7
CHAPTER	II	9
CHAPTER	III	19
CHAPTER	IV	27
CHAPTER	V	33
CHAPTER	VI	39
CHAPTER	VII	45
CHAPTER	VIII	54
CHAPTER	IX	63
CHAPTER	X	72
CHAPTER	XI	86
CHAPTER	XII	96
CHAPTER	XIII	114
CHAPTER	XIV	123
CHAPTER	XV	130
CHAPTER	XVI	143
CHAPTER	XVII	154
CHAPTER	XVIII	164
CHAPTER	XIX	173

CHAPTER	XX	. . . .	182
CHAPTER	XXI	. . . .	191
CHAPTER	XXII	. . . .	202
CHAPTER	XXIII	. . . .	208
CHAPTER	XXIV	. . . .	219
CHAPTER	XXV	. . . .	229
CHAPTER	XXVI	. . . .	234
CHAPTER	XXVII	. . . .	244
CHAPTER	XXVIII	. . . .	256
CHAPTER	XXIX	. . . .	262
CHAPTER	XXX	. . . .	270
CHAPTER	XXXI	. . . .	279
EPILOGUE		. . . .	283

CHAPTER I

Martin Fawley glanced irritably at the man stretched flat in the chair he coveted—the man whose cheeks were partly concealed by lather, and whose mass of dark hair was wildly disarranged. One of his hands—delicate white hands they were although the fingers were long and forceful—reposed in a silver bowl of hot water. The other one was being treated by the manicurist seated on a stool by his side, the young woman whose services Fawley also coveted. He had entered the establishment a little abruptly and he stood with his watch in his hand. Even Fawley's friends did not claim for him that he was a good-tempered person.

"Monsieur is ten minutes *en retard*," the coiffeur announced with a reproachful gesture.

"Nearly a quarter of an hour," the manicurist echoed with a sigh.

The new-comer replaced his watch. The two statements were incontrovertible. Nevertheless, the ill humour which he felt was eloquently reflected in his face. The man in the chair looked at him expressionless, indifferent. The inconvenience of a stranger meant nothing to him.

"If Monsieur will seat himself," Henri, the coiffeur, suggested, "this will not be a long affair."

Fawley glanced once more at his watch. He really had nothing whatever to do at the moment, but he possessed all the impatience of the man of energy at being asked to wait at any time. While he seemed to be considering the situation the man in the chair spoke. His French was good enough, but it was not the French of a native.

"It would be a pity," he said, "that Monsieur should be misled. I require *ensuite* a face massage, and I am not satisfied with the hands which Mademoiselle thinks she has finished. Furthermore, there is the trimming of my eyebrows—a delicate task which needs great care."

Martin Fawley stared at the speaker rudely.

"So you mean to spend the morning here," he observed.

The man in the chair glanced at Fawley nonchalantly and remained silent. Fawley turned his back upon him, upon Henri, and Mathilde, the white painted furniture, the glittering mirrors, and walked out into the street.... He did not see again this man to whom he had taken so unreasonable a dislike until he was ushered, a few days later, with much ceremony into his very magnificent official apartment in the Plaza Margaretta at Rome.

CHAPTER II

GENERAL BERATI looked at his visitor, as he motioned to a chair, with very much the same stony indifference with which he had regarded him in the barber's shop at Nice. Their eyes met and they exchanged one long, calculating glance. Fawley felt the spell of the man from that moment. Often afterwards he wondered why he had not felt it even when he had seen him with his face half covered with lather and his fingers plunged into the silver bowl.

"You have come direct from Paris?" Berati asked.

"Those were my instructions. I was at your Embassy on Thursday afternoon. I caught the Rome express at seven o'clock."

"You have an earnest sponsor in Paris?"

"Carlo Antonelli. I have worked with him."

"So I understand. Why are you not working for your own country?"

"There are half a dozen more of us Americans to whom you might address that question," Fawley explained. "The department to which I belong has been completely disbanded. M.I.B.C. exists no longer."

"You mean," Berati asked, with a keen glance from under his bushy black eyebrows, "that your country has no longer a Secret Service?"

"It amounts to that," Fawley admitted. "Our present-day politicians believe that all information acquired through Secret Service work is untrustworthy and dangerous. They have adopted new methods."

"So you are willing to work for another country?"

"Provided," Fawley stipulated, "I am assured that the work does not conflict directly with American or British interests."

"The Americans," Berati observed quietly, "are the only people who have no idea what their real interests are."

"In what respect?"

The Italian shrugged his shoulders very slightly.

"America," he said, "needs the information which Secret Service agents could afford them as much or more than any nation in the world. However, you need have no fear nor need you think that you are the only foreigner who is working for us. You will probably become acquainted before your work is over with a German, a Monegasque and a Dane. I am not a believer in using one's own country-people exclusively."

"You strip our profession of its honourable side," Fawley remarked dryly. "That does not refer to myself. I am admittedly a free lance. I must have work of an adventurous type, and since my country cannot offer it to me I must seek for it in any decent way."

"Patriotism," Berati sneered, "has been the excuse for many a career of deceit."

"It has also been its justification," Fawley ventured.

Berati's expression did not change an iota, yet somehow his visitor was made to feel that he was not accustomed to argument.

"The present work is worth while for its own sake," he announced. "It is so dangerous that you might easily lose your life within a fortnight. That is why I shall give you out your work chapter by chapter. To-day I propose only to hand you your credentials—which by the by will mean sudden death to you if ever they are found by the wrong people upon your person—and explain the commencement of your task."

Berati touched a concealed bell embedded in the top of his desk. Almost immediately, through a door which Fawley had not previously noticed, a young man entered, noiseless and swift in his movements and of intriguing personality. His head was shaven like the head of a monk, his complexion was almost ivory white, unrelieved by the slightest tinge of colour. His fingers were bony. His frame was thin. The few words he addressed to his chief were spoken in so low a tone that, although Fawley's hearing was good and Italian the same to him as most other languages, he heard nothing. To his surprise Berati introduced the new-comer.

"This is my secretary, Prince Patoni," he said. "Major Fawley."

The young man bowed and held out his hand. Fawley found it, as he had expected, as cold as ice.

"Major Fawley's work was well known to us years ago," he remarked a little grimly. "As a confrère he will be welcome."

Almost immediately, in obedience to a gesture from Berati, he departed, leaving behind him a sense of unreality as though he were some phantom flitting across the stage of life rather than a real human being. But then indeed on that first day Berati himself seemed unreal to his visitor. The former tore open one of the packages and tossed its contents over the table.

"Open that," he directed.

Fawley obeyed. Inside was a plain platinum and gold cigarette case with six cigarettes on either side neatly kept in place by a platinum clasp.

"Well?" Berati demanded.

"Is that a challenge?" Fawley asked.

"You may accept it as such."

Fawley held the case with its diagonal corners between two fingers and ran the forefinger of his other hand backwards and forwards over the hinges. Almost instantaneously a third division of the case disclosed itself. Berati's expression remained unchanged, but his eyebrows were slowly and slightly elevated.

"There are three of you alive then," he remarked coolly. "I thought that there were only two."

"You happen to be right," his visitor told him. "Joseffi died very suddenly."

"When?"

"The day after he opened the case."

Berati, who indulged very seldom in gestures, touched his underlip with his long firm forefinger.

"Yet—you came."

Fawley smiled—perhaps a little sardonically.

"The men who work for you, General," he observed, "should rid themselves of any fear of death."

Berati nodded very slowly and very thoughtfully. He seemed to be appraising the man who stood on the other side of his desk.

"It appears to me," he admitted, "that we may get on."

"It is possible," Fawley agreed. "Curiosity prompts me to ask you one question, however. When you sent for me had you any idea that we had met in that barber's shop at Nice?"

"I knew it perfectly well."

"I confess that that puzzles me a little," Fawley admitted. "I was at my worst that day. I did not show the self-control of a schoolboy. I had not even the excuse of being in a hurry. I was annoyed because you had taken my place, and I showed it."

Berati smiled.

"It was the very fact," he pronounced, "that you were able to forget your profession on an ordinary occasion which commended you to me. Our own men—most of them at any rate—err on the side of being too stealthy. They are too obvious in their subterfuges ever to reach the summits. You have the art—or shall I call it the genius?—of being able to display your natural feelings when you are, so to speak, in mufti. You impressed me, as you would any man, with the idea that you were a somewhat choleric, somewhat crude Englishman or American, thinking as usual that the better half of any deal should fall to you. I made up my mind that if you were free you were my man."

"You had the advantage of me," Fawley reflected.

"I never forget a face," the other confided. "You were in Rome five years ago—some important mission—but I could recall it if I chose.... To proceed. You know where to look for your identification papers if it should become necessary to show them. Your supplementary passports are in the same place—both diplomatic and social."

"Passports," Fawley remarked, as he disposed of the cigarette case in the inner pocket of his waistcoat, "generally indicate a journey."

Berati's long fingers played for a moment with the stiff collar of his uniform. He looked meaningly across his table.

"Adventure is to be found in so many of these southern cities," he observed. "Monte Carlo is very pleasant at this time of the year and 'The France' is an excellent hotel. A countryman of ours, I remind myself, is in charge there. There is also a German named Krust—but that will do later. Our relations with him are at present undetermined. Your first centre of activities will be within twenty kilometres of the Casino. *A rivederci, signor.*"

He held out his hand. Fawley took it, but lingered for a moment.

"My instructions——" he began.

"They will arrive," the Italian interrupted. "Have no anxiety. There will be plenty of work for you. You will begin where Joseffi left off. I wish you better fortune."

Fawley obeyed the little wave of the hand and took his leave. In doing so, however, he made a not incomprehensible error. The room was irregular in shape, with panelled walls, and every one of the oval recesses possessed a door which matched its neighbour. His fingers closed upon the handle of the one through which he believed that he had entered. Almost at once Berati's voice snapped out from behind him like a pistol shot.

"Not that one! The next to your right."

Fawley did not, however, at once withdraw his hand from the beautiful piece of brass ornamentation upon which it rested.

"Where does this one lead to?" he asked with apparent irrelevance.

Berati's voice was suddenly harsh.

"My own apartments—the Palazzo Berati. Be so good as to pass out by the adjoining door."

Fawley remained motionless. Berati's voice was coldly angry.

"There is perhaps some explanation——" he began ominously.

"Explanation enough," Fawley interrupted. "Someone is holding the handle of this door on the other side. They are even now matching the strength of their fingers against mine."

"You mean that someone is attempting to enter?"

"Obviously," Fawley replied. "Shall I let them in?"

"In ten seconds," Berati directed. "Count ten to yourself and then open the door."

Fawley obeyed his new chief literally and it was probably that instinct of self-preservation which had always been helpfully present with him in times of crisis which saved his life. He sprang on one side, sheltering himself behind the partially opened door. A bullet whistled past his ear so that for hours afterwards he felt a singing there as though a hot wind was stabbing at him. There was a crash from behind in the room. Berati's chair was empty! Down the passage was dimly visible the figure of a woman, whose feet

seemed scarcely to touch the polished oak floor. Fawley
was barely in time, for she had almost reached the far end
before he started in pursuit. He called out to her, hoping
that she would turn her head and allow him a glimpse of her
face, but she was too clever for any *gaucherie* of that sort.
He passed through a little unseen cloud of faint, indefinite
perfume such as might float from a woman's handkerchief
shaken in the dark, stooped in his running to pick up and
thrust a glittering trifle into his pocket, and almost reached
her before she disappeared through some thickly hanging
brocaded curtains. It was only a matter of seconds before
Fawley flung them on one side in pursuit and emerged into
a large square ante-room with shabby magnificent hangings,
but with several wonderful pictures upon the walls, and
two closed doors on either side. He paused to listen, but all
that he could hear was the soft sobbing of stringed instru-
ments in the distance and a murmur of many voices apparently from the reception rooms of the Palazzo. He looked
doubtfully at the doors. They had the air of not having been
opened for generations. The only signs of human life came
from the corridor straight ahead which obviously led into
the reception rooms. Fawley hesitated only for a moment,
then he made his way cautiously along it until he arrived at a
slight bend and a further barrier of black curtains—curtains
of some heavy material which looked like velvet—embla-
zoned in faded gold with the arms of a famous family.... He

paused once more and listened. At that moment the music ceased. From the storm of applause he gathered that there must be at least several hundred people quite close to him on the other side of the curtain. He hesitated, frowning. Notwithstanding his eagerness to track down the would-be assassin, it seemed hopeless to make his way amongst a throng of strangers, however ingenious the explanations he might offer, in search of a woman whose face he had scarcely seen and whom he could recognise only by the colour of her gown. Reluctantly he retraced his steps and stood once more in the ante-room which, like many apartments in the great Roman palaces which he had visited, seemed somehow to have lost its sense of habitation and to carry with it a suggestion of disuse. There were the two doors. He looked at them doubtfully. Suddenly one was softly opened and a woman stood looking out at him with a half-curious, half-frightened expression in her brown eyes. She was wearing a dress the colour of which reminded him of the lemon groves around Sorrento.

CHAPTER III

AN angry and a frightened woman. Fawley had seen many of them before in his life but never quite one of this type. Her eyes, which should have been beautiful, were blazing. Her lips—gashes of scarlet fury—seemed as if they were on the point of withering him up with a storm of words. Yet when she spoke she spoke with reserve, without subtlety, a plain blunt question.

"Why are you following me about?"

"Scarcely that," he protested. "I am keeping you under observation for a time."

"Like all you Anglo-Saxons you are a liar and an impudent one," she spat out.... "Wait!"

Her tone had suddenly changed to one of alarm. Instinctively he followed her lead and listened. More and more distinctly he could hear detached voices at the end of the corridor which led into the reception rooms. The curtains must have been drawn on one side, for the hum of conversation became much louder. She caught at his wrist.

"Follow me," she ordered.

They passed into a darkened entresol. She flung open an inner door and Fawley found himself in a bedroom—a woman's bedroom—high-ceilinged, austere after the Italian fashion, but with exquisite linen and lace upon the old four-postered bed, and with a shrine in one corner, its old gilt work beautifully fashioned—a representation of the Madonna—a strangely moving work of art. She locked the door with a ponderous key.

"Is that necessary?" Fawley asked.

She scoffed at him. Fear had driven the fury from her face, and Fawley in an impersonal sort of way was beginning to realise how beautiful she was.

"Do not think that I am afraid," she said coldly. "I have done that to protect myself. If you refuse to give me what I ask for I shall shoot you and point to the locked door as my excuse. You followed me in. There can be no denying that."

She was passionately in earnest, but a sense of humour which had befriended Fawley in many grimmer moments chose inappropriately enough to assert itself just then. With all her determination it was obvious that her courage was a matter of nerve, that having once keyed herself up to a desperate action she was near enough now to collapse. Probably that made her the more dangerous, but Fawley did not stop to reflect. He leaned against the high-backed chair and laughed quietly.... Afterwards he realised that he was in as great danger of his life in those few seconds as at any time during his adventurous career. But after that first flash of renewed fury something responsive, or at any rate sympathetic, seemed to creep into her face and showed itself suddenly in the quivering of her lips. Her fingers, which had been creeping towards the bosom of her dress, retreated empty.

"Tell me what it is that you want from me," Fawley asked.

"You know," she answered. "I want my slipper."

He felt in his pocket and knew at once that his first suspicion had been correct. He shook his head gravely.

"Alas," he replied, "I am forced to keep this little memento of your expedition for the present. As to what happened a few minutes ago——"

"Well, what are you going to do about that?" she interrupted. "I deny nothing. I tried to kill Berati. But for the fact that you unnerved me—I did not expect to find anyone holding the door on the other side—I should have done it. As it is, I fear that he has escaped."

"What did you want to kill the General for?" Fawley asked curiously. "You are both Italian, are you not, and Berati is at least a patriot?"

"Take my advice," she answered, "and do not try to interfere in matters of which you know nothing."

"That seems a little hard upon me," Fawley protested with a smile. "I have been knocking about Europe for a reasonable number of years and I should say that no man had worked harder for his country than Berati."

"Nevertheless," she rejoined, "he is on the point of making a hideous blunder. If you had known as much as I do you would have stepped back and let me kill him."

"I am not in favour of murder as an argument," Fawley objected.

"You think too much of human life, you Americans," she scoffed.

"In any case Berati has done a great deal for Italy," he reminded her.

"There are some who think otherwise," she answered.

She listened for another moment, then she moved to the door and turned the key. She swung round and faced Fawley. The anger had all gone. Her eyes had softened. There was a note almost of pleading in her tone.

"There shall be no more melodrama," she promised. "I want what you picked up of mine. It is necessary that I go back to the reception of the Principessa."

"I am not detaining you," Fawley ventured to remind her hopefully.

"Do you suggest then," she asked, with a faint uplifting of her delicate eyebrows, "that I make my appearance in that crowded room with but one shoe on?"

"This being apparently your bedchamber," Fawley replied, looking round, "it occurs to me as possible that you might find another pair."

"Nothing that would go with the peculiar shade of my frock and these stockings," she assured him, lifting her skirt a few inches and showing him her exquisitely sheened ankles.

Fawley sighed.

"Alas," he regretted, "an hour ago I was a free man. You could have had your slipper with pleasure. At this moment

I am under a commitment to Berati. His interests and his safety—if he is still alive—must be my first consideration."

"Do you think that after all I hit him?" she asked eagerly.

"I fear that it is quite possible. All I know is that he was seated in his chair one moment, you fired, and when I looked round the chair was empty."

She smiled doubtfully.

"He is very hard to kill."

"And it appears to me that you are a very inexperienced assassin!"

"That," she confided, "is because I never wanted to kill a man before. Please give me my slipper."

He shook his head.

"If Berati is alive," he warned her, "it will be my duty to hand it over to him and to describe you according to the best of my ability."

"And if he is dead?"

"If he is dead my contract with him is finished and I shall leave Rome within an hour. You at any rate would be safe."

"How shall you describe me if you have to?" she asked with a bewildering smile.

Insouciance was a quality which Fawley, in common with most people, always admired in criminals and beautiful women. He tried his best with a clumsier tongue to follow her lead.

"Signorina," he said, "or Mademoiselle—heaven help me if I can make up my mind as to your nationality—I am afraid that my description would be of very little real utility because I cannot imagine myself inventing phrases to describe you adequately."

"That is quite good," she approved, "for a man in conference with a would-be murderess. But after all I must look like something or other."

"I will turn myself into a police proclamation," he announced. "You have unusual eyes which are more normal now but which a few minutes ago were shooting lightnings of hate at me. They are a very beautiful colour—a kind of hazel, I suppose. You have an Italian skin, the ivory pallor of perfect health which belongs only to your country-people. Your hair I should rather like to feel, but it looks like silk and it reminds one of dull gold. You have the figure of a child, but it is obvious that you have the tongue, the brain, the experience of a woman who has seen something of life.... With that description published would you dare to walk the streets of Rome to-morrow?"

"A proud woman but, alas, I fear in perfect safety," she sighed. "Too many people have failed with Berati and you distracted my attention. I saw his still, terrible face, but when I looked and hoped for that transforming cloud of horror I saw only you. You frightened me and I fled."

Fawley moved slightly towards the door.

"It is plainly my duty," he said, "to find out whether Berati is alive or dead."

"I agree with you."

"And when I have discovered?"

"Listen," she begged, moving a little nearer towards him. "There is a tiny café in a fashionable but not too reputable corner of Rome in the arcade leading from the Plaza Vittoria. Its name is 'the Café of the Shining Star.' You will find me there at ten o'clock. May I have my shoe so that I can make a dignified departure?"

Fawley shook his head. He pointed to an antique Italian armoire which looked as if it might have been a boot cupboard.

"You can help yourself, Signorina. The slipper I have in my pocket I keep until I know whether Berati is alive or dead."

"You keep it as evidence—yes? You would hand me over as the assassin? As though anyone would believe your story!"

"All the same," Fawley reminded her, "for the moment Berati is my master."

He turned the handle of the door. She kissed the tips of her fingers to him lightly.

"I can see," she sighed, "that you are one of those who do not change their minds. All the same I warn you there is danger in what you are doing."

"A slipper," Fawley protested, "a delicate satin slipper with a slightly raised inner sole could never bring me ill-luck."

She shook her head and there was no ghost of a smile upon her lips just now.

"Medici buckles," she confided. "They are very nearly priceless. Men and women in the old days paid with their lives for what you are doing."

Fawley smiled.

"You shall have the buckle back," he promised. "For the rest I will use my penknife carefully."

CHAPTER IV

ONCE more Fawley entered Berati's palatial bureau with a certain trepidation. His heart sank still further after his first glance towards the desk. The chair behind it was occupied by Prince Patoni.

"What about the Chief?" Fawley asked eagerly. "Was he hurt?"

The young man remained silent for a moment, his jet black eyes fixed upon his visitor's, his fingers toying with the watch-chain which was suspended from a high button of his waistcoat. He seemed, in his raven-like black clothes, with his hooked nose, his thin aristocratic face and bloodless lips, like some bird of prey.

"Our chief," he announced calmly, "is unhurt. A modern assassin seldom succeeds in checking a really great career. He has left a message for you. Will you be pleased to receive it?"

Fawley drew a sigh of relief. Life seemed suddenly to become less complicated.

"Let me hear what it is, if you please," he begged.

"The Chief has been summoned to his wife, the Principessa's, reception at the Palazzo. Some Royalties, I believe, have made their appearance. It is his wish that you should repair there immediately. Here," he added, pushing a highly glazed and beautifully engraved card across the table towards him, "is your invitation, as you are probably unknown to the servants and ushers of the household."

Fawley glanced at the card and thrust it into his pocket.

"I will go, of course," he replied, "but please explain to me how it is that Berati's wife is Principessa? He himself, I understood, had no other rank than his military one of General."

"That is quite true," Patoni admitted, "but our illustrious chief married some time ago the Principessa de Morenato.... You will leave the bureau as you entered it. When you reach the street turn to the right twice, and the entrance to the Palazzo courtyard confronts you. I must beg you not to delay."

"Tell me before I leave," Fawley begged, "if any orders have been issued for the arrest of the person who fired that shot?"

"The matter does not come, sir, within the scope of your activities," was the icy reply.

Fawley took his departure and made his way according to directions to where under a scarlet awning guests were coming and going from the great grey stone Palazzo. A very courtly seneschal received his card with enthusiasm, and conducted him into a magnificent room still filled with men and women talking together in animated groups, dancing in a further apartment, or listening to soft music in a still more distant one. He led Fawley towards a slightly raised floor, and in a tone which he contrived to make almost reverential announced the visitor. The Principessa, a handsome woman of the best Roman type, gave him her lifted fingers and listened agreeably to his few words.

"My husband has told me of your coming," she confided. "It will give him pleasure before you leave to have a further word with you. He is showing one of the Royal Princes who have honoured us with their presence a famous Murillo which came into our family a short time ago.... Elida, do not tell me that you are going to leave us so soon?"

Fawley glanced around. Some instinct had already told him whom he would find standing almost at his elbow. It seemed to him, however, that he had not realised until that moment in the overheated, flower-scented room with its soft odours of femininity, its vague atmosphere of sensuous disturbance, the full subtlety of her attraction. The tension which had somewhat hardened her features a few minutes ago had gone. An air of gentle courtesy had taken its place. She smiled as though the impending introduction would be a pleasure to her.

"It is Major Martin Fawley, an American of many distinctions which for the moment I cannot call to mind," the Princess said. "My, alas, rather distant relative the Princess Elida di Rezco di Vasena."

The formal introduction with its somewhat Italian vagueness gave Fawley no hint as to whether the Princess were married or not, so he contented himself with a ceremonious bow. He murmured some commonplace to which she replied in very much the same fashion. Then a new-comer presented himself to the Princess and the latter turned away to greet him. Fawley found himself involuntarily glancing at his companion's feet. She was elegantly shod in bronze slippers, but the bronze and the lemon colour were not an ideal combination.

"It is your fault," she reminded him gently. "In a short time I hope that you will see me properly shod. Tell me your news. There seem to be no rumours about."

Her coolness was almost repelling, and Fawley felt himself relieved by the gleam of anxiety in her eyes. The reply, however, which was framing upon his lips became unnecessary. It seemed as though both became aware of a certain fact at the same moment. Within a few feet of them, but so placed that he was not directly in their line of vision, stood the man whom all Italy was beginning to fear. General Berati, very impressive in his sombre uniform, very much alive, was watching the two with steady gaze.

"Princess," Fawley said, determined to break through the tenseness of those few seconds, "I am wondering whether I have had the happiness to meet one of your family. There was a di Vasena riding some wonderful horses in the show at San Remo last year. I met him at a friendly game of polo afterwards."

"My brother," she exclaimed, with a quick smile of appreciation. "I am glad that you remembered him. He is my favourite in the family. You are like all your country-people, I suppose, and the English too, very fond of games."

"We have less opportunity nowadays for indulging in them," Fawley regretted.

"You would say that I speak in—what is the English word?—platitudes if I suggested that you had been driven to the greater amusements?"

"There is truth in the idea at any rate," Fawley admitted.

She turned and touched the arm of a young uniformed soldier who was standing near by.

"You remember Major Fawley, Antonio?" she asked. "He met you——"

"Why, at San Remo. Naturally I do," the young man interrupted. "We played polo afterwards. The Ortini found us ponies and I remember, sir," he went on, with a smile, "that you showed us how Americans can ride."

"I shall leave you two together for a time," Elida announced. "I have to make my adieux. Rome is suffering just now, as your witty Ambassador remarked the other day," she observed, "from an epidemic of congested hospitality. Everyone is entertaining at the same time."

She passed on, made her curtsy to royalty, and lingered for a moment with her hostess. Fawley exchanged a few commonplaces with di Vasena and afterwards took his leave. He looked everywhere for his chief, but Berati was nowhere to be found. It seemed almost as though he had sprung out of the earth to watch the meeting between his would-be assassin and Fawley, and then, having satisfied himself, disappeared.

CHAPTER V

THE Café of the Shining Star could have existed nowhere but in Rome, and nowhere in Rome but in that deserted Plaza Vittoria with its strange little pool of subdued lights. Its decorations were black, its furniture dingy but reminiscent of past magnificence. A broad staircase ascended from the middle of the sparsely occupied restaurant, and from the pillars supporting it were suspended two lights enclosed in antique lanterns. As Fawley entered a weary-looking maître d'hôtel came forward, bowed and without wasting words pointed to the stairs.

Madame, the *patrona*, from behind a small counter where with her head supported between her hands she studied the pages of her ledger, also glanced up and with a welcoming smile pointed upwards. Fawley mounted the stairs to a room in which barely a dozen people were seated at small tables—people of a class whom for the moment he found it difficult to place. At the further end of the room, at a table encircled by a ponderous screen, he found the Princess. A dour-looking woman standing patiently by her side fell back on his arrival.

"Sit down if you please, Major Fawley," Elida begged him. "I have ordered wine. You see it here. Drink a glass of it or not as you please. It is very famous—it has been in the cellars of this café for more years than I have lived—or perhaps you."

Fawley obeyed her gestured invitation, seated himself opposite to her and poured out two glasses of the clear amber wine. She laughed a toast across at him.

"You come in a good humour, I trust," she said. "You know at least that I am not an ordinary assassin. Perhaps I am sorry already that I raised my hand against my relation-in-law. He is on the point, I fear, of making a great mistake, but to kill—well, perhaps I was wrong."

"I am very glad to hear you say so," Fawley murmured.

"You have brought the slipper?"

"I have brought the slipper," he acknowledged. "It has, in fact, never left my possession."

"You will give it to me?" she exclaimed, holding out her hand.

"Yes, I will give it to you," Fawley assented.

The tips of her fingers tapped hard against the table cloth.

"I cannot wait," she prayed. "Give it to me now."

"There are terms," Fawley warned her.

Disappointment shone out of her eyes. Her lips quivered. For a moment his attention wandered. He was thinking that her mouth was the most exquisite thing he had ever seen. He was wondering——

"Do not keep me in suspense, please," she begged. "What terms do you speak of?"

"You will not find them difficult," he assured her, "especially as you have confessed just now that you are not an assassin at heart. Listen to my proposition."

"Proposition," she sighed, her eyes once more dancing. "I am intrigued. Will you commence? I am all eagerness."

"Fold your hands in front of your bosom and swear to me that you will not repeat this afternoon's adventure and you shall have your slipper."

She held out her hands.

"Please place them exactly as you desire."

Fawley crossed them. Like white flowers they were—soft and fragrant, with nails showing faintly pink underneath, but innocent of any disfiguring stain of colour. She repeated after him the few words which form the sacred oath of the Roman woman. When she had finished she treated him to a little grimace.

"You are too clever, my chivalrous captor," she complained. "Fancy your being able to play the priest. And now, please, the slipper."

Fawley drew it from his pocket and laid it upon the table. The exquisite paste buckle with the strangely set crown flamed out its brilliant colouring into the room.

"You regret the buckle?" she asked. "It is very beautiful and very valuable. It is quite authentic, too. There is Medici blood in my veins. That, I suppose, is why I have the impulse to kill!"

A single lamp stood upon the table with a worn shade of rose-coloured silk. Except for its rather fantastic and very dim illumination they sat amongst the shadows. Her hand touched his, which still rested upon the slipper.

"You will give it to me?" she whispered.

"I shall give it to you," Fawley agreed, "but do not please think that the buckle or even the fact that you have worn it are the only things I have found precious."

"What do you mean?" she asked fearfully.

Fawley lifted the delicate innersole of the slipper and looked up. Their eyes met across the table. She was breathing quickly.

"You have read it?" she gasped.

"Naturally."

"You are keeping it?"

"On the contrary, I am returning it to you."

A wave of relief drove the tension from her face. She seemed for the moment speechless. The paper which he handed across the table found its way almost mechanically into the jewelled handbag by her side.

"At the same time," he went on gravely, "you must not hope for too much. I am in the service of Berati. I must tell him what I found in the slipper of the woman who tried to kill him."

"You will tell him who it was?"

"I think that I am wrong, but that I propose to forget," he told her. "You have probably made many men forget themselves in your brief years, Princess. You will make many more. What I read I shall communicate to Berati. The source of my information I shall keep to myself. Take the slipper."

Her hands were drawing it off the table, but as though by accident they passed over Fawley's and he felt their shivering warmth. There was a softer light in her eyes than he had ever seen.

"Princess—Elida——" he whispered.

She leaned towards him, but Fawley swung suddenly round in his chair. Patoni, stark and sinister, was standing by the side of the screen, looking in. His smile was one of composed malevolence.

"I beg a thousand pardons," he apologised, with a stiff little bow. "I am here on a mission of great importance."

Fawley rose to his feet. He was as tall as Patoni and at that moment his face was as hard and set.

"It is part of your Italian manners," he asked, "to play the spy in this way?"

"I have offered you my apologies," was the cold retort. "A quarrel between us is not possible, Major Fawley. I am still of the Church and I do not fight duels. I am compelled to ask you to accompany me without a moment's delay to the Generalissimo."

"The Princess——" Fawley began.

"Has her duenna," Patoni interrupted.

Elida leaned forward and suddenly clasped Fawley's hand. He seemed somehow to have grown in stature, a man on fire with anger and without a doubt dangerous. Even the two carabinieri standing behind Patoni looked at him with respect.

"Please go," she begged. "Please go with Prince Patoni, my friend. My car is waiting, my servant is here. I need no escort. I wish so much that you do as I ask."

Fawley bent over her hands and touched them with his lips. Then he turned and left the room with Patoni.

CHAPTER VI

In a life full of surprises Martin Fawley was inclined to doubt whether he ever received a greater one than when, for the second time during the same day, he was ushered into the presence of General Berati, the most dreaded man in Rome. Gone was the severe high-necked and tight-waisted uniform, gone the iciness of his speech and the cold precision of his words. It was a tolerable imitation of a human being with whom Fawley was confronted—a dark-haired, undersized but sufficiently good-looking man dressed in a suit of apparently English tweeds, stretched at his full length upon the sofa of a comfortable sitting-room leading out of his bureau, reading the *New York Herald* and with something that looked suspiciously like a Scotch whisky and soda by his side. He threw down his paper and welcomed his visitor with a grim cordiality.

"Come in, Major," he invited. "I will offer you a whisky and soda as soon as you tell me exactly whom you found on the other side of that door."

Fawley accepted the chair to which his host had pointed.

"May I take the liberty," he begged, "of asking a question first?"

"Why not?" Berati answered with unabated good-humour. "This is an unofficial conversation. Proceed."

"Where did you disappear to after that first shot?"

Berati chuckled.

"I give audiences too easily," he confided, "and for that reason I have several little contrivances of my own invention. Some day I will show you this one. There is a button on my desk which I touch, the rubber floor upon which I sit disappears, and so do I, into the room below. I should explain perhaps that it is only a drop of a few feet and the end is what you call in England a feather bed. And now the answer to my question, please."

Martin Fawley was probably as near complete embarrassment as ever before in his life. He hated the position in which he found himself. He hated what he was about to do. He kept his countenance, but he was bitterly mortified as he felt for a secret pocket inside his coat and silently withdrew his cigarette case.

"General Berati," he said, "I feel thoroughly ashamed of myself and I shall merit what you will doubtless think of me. At the same time do remember this—I am to some extent a mercenary in your service. I allow myself that amount of excuse. It was a woman who fired the shot and, as you see, I am handing back my papers."

"This is most intriguing," Berati observed. "I gather then that you refuse to tell me her name?"

"Frankly," Fawley replied, "I believe you know it already, but all the same you are right: I refuse to tell you her name.

I have been in your service for the matter of a few hours, I see you nearly killed, I know who fired the shot and I am not going to tell you who it was."

"Capital," Berati exclaimed. "Just what I should have expected from you. Put back your cigarette case, my young friend. After all, you probably saved my life, for, thanks to you, there was no second shot."

"You know who it was?" Fawley asked, a little bewildered.

"Perfectly well," Berati confided. "I joined my wife's guests," he went on, "chiefly for the pleasure of seeing whether you showed any embarrassment when you were presented to a certain one of our Roman beauties. My congratulations, Major. You have some, at any rate, of the gifts necessary in our profession. Let me offer you a whisky and soda. You see, I am a great admirer of your country and I try even to adopt her drinks."

Fawley thanked him and helped himself. Berati's intonation as well as his manner seemed to have become curiously Anglo-Saxon.

"Listen, my friend," he continued. "When an attempt is made upon my life I never, if I can help it, allow anything to appear in the journals. You do not wish to give away a beautiful lady any more than I want to admit to the indignity of having been nearly wiped off the earth by so frail an instrument."

"I think, sir, that you are a very brave and a very forgiving man," Fawley declared, with an impulsiveness which was absolutely foreign to his character.

Berati laughed almost gaily.

"No man," he said, "who is in touch with the great affairs of the world can afford to be made ridiculous. An attempt on my life by my wife's niece, by the Princess Elida, is a thing to smile at. Nevertheless," he went on, his tone becoming a trifle graver, "I have reason to believe that the Princess was carrying with her a paper of some importance."

"She was," Fawley admitted.

"You discovered it?" Berati snapped out, with a trace of his former manner.

"I discovered it," Fawley confessed. "Its purport is at your disposal."

"And the paper?"

"I returned it to the Princess."

Berati's air of bonhomie temporarily disappeared. He scowled.

"An amazing act of gallantry at my expense," he sneered.

"Bad enough in my position, I admit, but not quite as bad as it seems," Fawley pointed out. "I have already told you that the purport of that paper is at your disposal."

"It was signed by one who used to bear a great name in Germany?" Berati asked.

"It was," Fawley assented.

"And in return for certain action on your part you were offered——?"

"I can tell you specifically if you like."

Berati shook his head.

"A copy of the proposed agreement reached me ten minutes ago. My mind is not made up. I have decided to wait until you have visited Germany. Your reports from there will influence me. At present I have an open mind. The Princess Elida has been bitterly disappointed," he went on, "by what she thought was a point-blank refusal on my part. She believes that I lean towards Behrling. She has the usual woman's fault—she jumps at conclusions."

"Is it permitted to ask what your intentions are with regard to the Princess?"

Berati grunted.

"Nothing venomous, I can assure you. I do not make war on women. She is now on her way to Vienna in the safest of my airships. I regret the necessity for such discipline, but she will not be allowed to cross the frontier again for a year. This need not disturb you, my friend, for I doubt whether you will spend much of your time in this country. You will recognise the fact, I am sure, that, however much I may choose to risk in the way of danger, I cannot afford to be made ridiculous."

"I think that you have behaved very generously," Fawley declared.

Berati rose to his feet and touched the bell.

"The car in which you arrived is waiting for you, Fawley," he announced. "Your place is taken in the night train for Monte Carlo. You have thirty-five minutes. Good luck to you. Carlo," he added in Italian to the servant who had answered the bell, "show this gentleman to his automobile. He goes to the Central Railway Station. By the by, Fawley, your luggage has all been registered, and your small things put in your compartment. Once more—good-night, and good luck to you."

Fawley lingered for a moment until the servant was out of hearing.

"How do you propose to communicate with me, General?" he asked.

"Concerning that you need not worry," was the bland reply. "I do not approve of the telephone or the telegraph, and I like even less letters which go through the post. Live your own perfectly natural life. Some day you will find in your salon a blue envelope."

CHAPTER VII

THE blue envelope!

Fawley threw down the tennis racket he had been carrying, turned the key in the lock of his sitting-room door at the Hôtel de France, and moved swiftly to the writing table on which the letter had been placed. He tore it open, read it very deliberately—for it was in a somewhat curious cipher which he had only just committed to memory—and then, lighting a match, watched it slowly consume to ashes. Afterwards he lingered for a few minutes on his balcony looking up towards the misty peaks eastwards of Mont Agel. He no longer regretted the fortnight's idleness, the non-appearance of Krust, the almost stagnant calm of his days. He had thoroughly established himself as a leisure-loving American with a passion for games. He now busied himself at the telephone cancelling a few social engagements, for Fawley, reserved though he was by habit, was a man always sought after.

"A few days' golf up at Sospel," he told everyone after he had packed his clothes.

He wondered a little grimly whither those few days' golf would lead him. Perhaps to the same place as Joseffi, who had been found in the gardens with a bullet through his heart and a revolver by his side, but who had never been known to enter the Casino in his life.

"You are not leaving us, sir?" the valet de chambre enquired as he answered the bell.

"Only for a few days," Fawley assured him. "I am keeping on my rooms."

"You are not leaving us, Major Fawley, I trust," the smiling and urbane manager asked him in the hall.

"Only for a few days," Fawley repeated. "I am going to explore your hills and try another golf links. Back about Sunday, I should think. Keep my letters."

"I wish you a pleasant and successful expedition," the manager remarked, with a final bow.

Fawley's smile was perhaps a little enigmatic. He waved his hand and drove off without further speech.

Fawley, some five days later, driving his high-powered Lancia car through one of the many passes of the Lesser Alps between Roquebrune and the frontier, suddenly swung round a corner to find himself confronted by a movable obstruction of white, freshly-painted rails and an ominous notice. A soldier in the uniform of the Chasseurs Alpins stepped forward, his rifle at a threatening angle.

"There is no road this way, Monsieur," he announced curtly.

Fawley, who had brought his car to a standstill, leaned forward and produced a map. He addressed the soldier in his own language.

"My young friend," he protested, "I fancy that you are mistaken. You have blocked the wrong road. This is clearly marked in the latest edition of the issued maps as a Number Two road between Hegel and the village of Les Estaples."

"Your map is of no consequence," the man replied. "This road was taken over by the military some time ago. There is no passage here for civilians."

A sergeant, who had been sitting on a rock amongst the sparse pine trees smoking a cigarette, scrambled down to them.

"What is the trouble?" he demanded.

"Monsieur desires to use this route," his subordinate confided. "I have told him that it exists now only for military purposes. He must return the way he came."

"*C'est exact*," the sergeant declared. "Where were you bound for by this route, Monsieur?"

Fawley leaned from his seat.

"I have been told," he replied confidentially, "that your army are thinking of erecting military works here. I wish to discover how far that is the truth."

The sergeant stared at him. So did the private. So did the young lieutenant who had just ridden up on a high-spirited horse in time to hear the end of the sentence.

"What is the reason for Monsieur's desire to gain this information?" he asked, wheeling round so that he completely blocked the road.

"I might reply that that is my affair," Fawley declared. "I really do not see why I should be questioned in this fashion. I have a map in my hand which clearly indicates this as a public thoroughfare."

The lieutenant made a sign. The sergeant mounted on one footboard, the private on the other.

"Go backwards in reverse," Fawley was ordered. "Take the narrow turning to the right about thirty metres back."

"Where will it lead me?" Fawley asked doubtfully.

"You will find out when you get there," was the curt reply. "If you hesitate I shall have to ask you to consider yourself under arrest."

Fawley, grumbling to himself all the time, obeyed orders. He found himself, after a climb of a couple of kilometres along a road which commenced in villainous fashion, but the latter portion of which was smooth and beautifully engineered, in front of a recently built white stone house around which a considerable clearing had been made. A sentry stood in front of the door. The lieutenant, who had galloped on ahead, had disappeared into the house. Fawley rose to his feet.

"Is this where I get out?" he asked.

"On the contrary, you remain where you are," the sergeant replied gruffly. "Our Lieutenant is now interviewing the Commandant."

Fawley lit a cigarette and gazed down the avenue of fallen pines to the broken country beyond, the bare peaks fading into the mist with the background of snow-capped ridges incredibly near.

"A trifle wild here," Fawley remarked. "You seem to have cut down a great many trees. You use a lot of timber in the army, I suppose."

The sergeant maintained a scornful silence. The private grinned. The horizon was suddenly blurred. A few flakes of sleet began to fall.

"Any objection to my putting up the hood?" Fawley asked, shivering.

The sergeant pointed to the house.

"You will be warm enough in there," he said. "Monsieur le Lieutenant is coming to fetch you."

The lieutenant approached them and motioned Fawley to descend.

"Colonel Dumesnil would like a word or two with you, Monsieur," he announced. "Will you be so good as to come this way? Sergeant!"

The sergeant's instructions were unspoken but obvious. He walked by Fawley's side, and the steel of his unsheathed bayonet was very much in evidence. Fawley turned up his coat collar and swore softly.

"I shall never find my way down through this labyrinth of passes if you keep me here much longer," he grumbled. "Why does your commandant wish to speak to me?"

"That you will soon discover," the lieutenant answered shortly. "Let me advise you to answer his questions politely and without complaint. The Colonel is not noted for his good temper. This way, please."

Fawley was ushered into what might have been an orderly-room. Colonel Dumesnil looked up from his task of studying a pile of maps and watched the new-comer keenly. The former was a short man whose spurred riding-boots scarcely reached the floor, but his face was stern and his steel grey eyes and tone were alike menacing.

"Will you explain, sir, what you are doing on a military reservation?" he demanded.

"I was following a road which is marked on my map as an ordinary civilian thoroughfare," Fawley explained. "I had a perfect right to be where I was."

"That, sir, one might easily dispute," was the cold reply. "All the roads round here are well known by the handful of scattered residents to be under military supervision. I must ask you what you are doing in this part of the world."

"There is no secret about it," Fawley answered blandly. "I have been trying to discover the extent and nature of the new French fortifications."

No more unexpected reply could have been given. There was a dead silence. The Colonel's face remained immovable, but there was an ominous tapping of his fingers upon the desk.

"For what reason?"

Fawley shrugged his shoulders.

"If you insist upon knowing I suppose I had better tell you," he said, "but I don't want the thing to get about. There are some golf links about twelve kilometres from here at a place called Sospel. I have taken a great fancy to them and to the hotel, and as I have a little capital to invest I thought of buying the lot. The one thing which makes me hesitate is that no one is willing or able to tell me where the new French fortifications and gun emplacements are situated, and until I know that I feel that my property might be utterly destroyed in case of war."

There was a further silence. Another officer who might have been the Colonel's aide-de-camp crossed the room and whispered in his ear.

"You have corroborative evidence of what you are telling me?" the Colonel asked.

"Any quantity," Fawley assured him confidently. "The Mayor of the district, the committee of the old golf club, the late hotel proprietor and owner of the land, half the village of Sospel."

"Your name and passport."

Fawley produced them from his pocket and handed them across. The Colonel examined them and his face relaxed.

"As an ex-military man, Major Fawley," he said, with a certain severity still in his tone, "you should have known that yours was a very dangerous enterprise. You should have applied to the authorities for any information you desired."

"I thought as mine was a civil enterprise," Fawley argued, "they might not notice me. All that I need is a little general information."

"There is none to be given," was the brusque reply. "Escort this gentleman to our boundaries, Lieutenant, and let me warn you, sir, not to be found in this locality again. This is from no lack of courtesy, Major Fawley. It is a matter of military necessity which I am amazed that you should not already have realised and respected."

Fawley suffered himself to be led away. A soldier escorted him to the nearest village, where he descended at the local café, and accepted without hesitation a ten-franc note to be spent there. He refused, however, to answer the slightest question respecting the geography of the neighbourhood and regarded with evident suspicion Fawley's few tentative enquiries.

"Monsieur has been generous," were his parting words as he stood outside the café. "He would be wise to listen to a word of advice. Strangers are sometimes treated generously, as Monsieur has been, on their first visit to the nest in the mountains. The second visit means the cold steel or the swift bullet. The bones of more than one too curious person will be found in the secret places of the mountains yonder when the world comes to an end."

He pointed up beyond the pass which they had descended. A stern, inhospitable line of country it was with great declivities and huge fragments of rock split by the slow fires of eternity. Fawley shivered a little as he stepped back into the car.

"I shall not forget, my brave fellow," he declared. "Drink a glass for me. I am best out of the neighbourhood."

The soldier grinned. Nevertheless, there was something serious in his expression behind the grin.

"*Monsieur est un homme prudent,*" was his only comment.

CHAPTER VIII

FAWLEY, a few nights later, lay on his stomach in the midst of a crumpled heap of undergrowth on almost the topmost spur of the range of mountains eastward from Mont Agel and very little below the snow line. He was on the edge of a recently made clearing and the air was full of the odour of the sawn pine trunks lying about in every direction. The mists rolled over his head and the frozen rain stung his cheeks and pattered against his leather clothes. It was the third moonless night of his almost concluded enterprise and there remained only one unsolved mystery. The six galleries were there visualised before his eyes. He knew the connecting points of each one and the whereabouts of most of the amazing battery of guns. He knew the entrances and roughly the exits to each. His work had been done with genius and good fortune, yet it was incomplete. The seventh gallery! The key to all the positions. The seventh gallery which must hold the wonder gun. Its exact whereabouts still eluded him.

The night before the storm which had swept the mountains bare, which had driven even the guards and sentries into shelter, had been a godsend to him. In the roar of the elements and that blinding deluge of rain, the crashing of the trees and the hissing of the wind through the undergrowth and along the ground, he had abandoned caution. He had tramped steadily round from post to post. He had been within a few yards of the Colonel's headquarters. He had even laid his hand on one of the guns, but it was not the gun he sought. He had worked it all out, though, by a process of elimination. The main gallery, the control station and the supreme mystery which was probably the mightiest antiaircraft gun in the world must be somewhere within a radius of about a hundred yards of where he was. It was information invaluable enough as it stood, but Fawley, through these long hours of darkness and peril, had conceived an almost passionate desire to solve the last enigma of this subterranean mountain fortress. The howling of the wind, which the night before had been his great aid, obscuring all sound and leaving him free to roam about in the darkness in comparative safety, was now, he felt, robbing him of his chance. The special body of men of whom he was in search—he had discovered that many hours ago—worked only in the darkness, so that even the woodcutters should know nothing of their doings. They must be somewhere near now.... There were great piles of cement half carted away lying within fifty feet of where he was, barrels of mortar, light and heavy trucks. Somewhere close to him they must be working.... This business of listening grew more hopeless. One of the trees in the wood, on the outskirts of which he lay, was creaking and roaring like a wild animal in pain. He raised himself slowly and carefully on one side and by straining his eyes he could catch the outlines of its boughs stretched out in fantastic fashion like great arms. He even heard the splinters go. Then, for the first time, he fancied he heard—not one voice but a hum of voices! His whole body stiffened—not with fear but with the realisation of danger. The voices seemed to come from below. He raised himself a little more almost on to his knees. His eyeballs burned with the agony of the fruitless effort to penetrate the darkness. Below! In his brain at any rate there was light enough. He remembered the somewhat artificial appearance of the great masses of undergrowth amongst which he lay. Perhaps this number seven tunnel was underneath! Perhaps in seeking for shelter he had crept into a ready made ambush. Then for some time he ceased to think and action became almost automatic.

Nothing in the orchestra of the howling wind, the crashing trees and the hollow echoes amongst the grim mountains had produced sound such as now seemed to split his ear-drums. Within a few feet of him there came a crash which blotted out the whole world with a great barrier of sound. He felt his cheeks whipped, his body thrashed, the sense of an earthquake underneath him—the sense of falling. It took him only a second or two to realise what was happening. Within a few yards of him the tree which he had been watching had given up its fight with the rising wind and had crashed through the artificial roof on which he lay, down into the space below. He, too, was falling as the branches and shrubs on either side subsided. He fell with his mind quite clear. He saw two men in the familiar uniform of the Chasseurs Alpins, their faces convulsed with amazed fear, flung to the ground by the trunk of the tree. It fell upon them so that Fawley, even in those wild seconds of excitement, was obliged to close his eyes. Their shrieking and yelling was all over in a moment.... Fawley himself fell sideways on to the platform of a smooth and shining cylindrical erection which was unlike anything he had ever seen before. There was nothing to which he could cling, and almost at once he slid down on to the cement floor. Opposite him was the most astonished human being he had ever seen—a soldier, who had run to the assistance of the other two and was suddenly faced with the consciousness of Fawley's amazing appearance.

"*Sacré nom de Dieu!*" he called out, wringing his hands. "What is it then that has arrived? Is it an earthquake? Who are you?"

"Never mind. Stay where you are. Don't raise your hands."

One last sobbing cry went down and echoed from wall to wall of the passage. Fawley took one look under the tree and then turned his back.

"They are dead," he said. "You cannot help them. Listen. Is this gallery number seven?"

The chasseur, incapable of speech, pointed to the wall. There it was—a great sprawling seven.

"Which is the way out?" Fawley asked.

The youth—he was scarcely more than a boy—was shivering so that words were almost impossible. He pointed in a certain direction. Fawley drew an automatic from his pocket.

"Look here," he threatened, "if you have lied, I shall come back and shoot you."

The chasseur pointed again. His face was white. He looked almost as though he had had a stroke. His head was bleeding where one of the boughs had struck him. The tree lay like a great destroying octopus all over the place. Only one thing seemed to have survived untouched. The great machine, with its metal cylinders and huge dynamos, which might well have been some devilish contrivance of the nether world.

"Where do you come from?" the youth asked.

Fawley raised his weapon. He had completely recovered his self-control.

"No more questions," he said curtly. "Give me your belt."

The soldier obeyed. Fawley's hand seemed as steady as a rock and the revolver, though small, was an ugly-looking affair.

"Put your hands out. Fold them together."

Again the chasseur obeyed. Fawley tied them, then, leaning forward, he struck him lightly but firmly near the chin.

"That is for your good," he said, as his victim stumbled backwards.

He turned away and crawled down the passage. There was no sentry, but the wind had ceased its sobbing for a moment and from the road came the sound of voices and the hurrying of feet. Fawley, bent double, made his way through the rough piece of waste ground towards the edge of the precipice. Something seemed to have created an alarm and shots came from behind him to which he paid no attention. A bullet whistled over his head. He only smiled. At the edge of the precipice he steadied himself: six hundred feet to scramble. Well, he had done it before. He fell flat just in time to escape another bullet and then, with gloved hands and his thick leather clothes, he commenced the wild descent. Sometimes his feet slipped and he heard the crashing of the small boulders and stones which he had dislodged. He felt himself falling through space, but each time a bump in the ground, or a bush, or a young pine sapling saved him. Once he hung over an absolutely sheer precipice, his legs dangling in the air, the trunk of the tree he clasped cracking and splintering in his hands. He pulled himself up again, made a little détour and felt the ground rise beneath his feet. As he descended lower and lower the wind and rain grew less, the cold decreased. The time came when he found himself standing upright on the solid earth. Below him long stretches of wood lay like black smudges of fallen clouds, but for a time at any rate he had reached a rough path down which he was able to scramble without difficulty. He took one pull at his flask and in a dark spot with trees all around one quick glance at his compass with the help of his torch. A sparsely planted wood was a godsend to him. He swung himself from trunk to trunk of the trees, his feet secure in the thick accumulation of pine needles below. When he emerged it was to face a flickering light from a small hamlet already astir. Before daybreak he was in his car clad in a rough knickerbocker suit, smoking a pipe, leaning nonchalantly back in his seat, and already well on his way down the great descent to the sea.

Monsieur Carlotti, the very popular manager of the Hôtel de France, was taking his usual morning promenade in the lounge of the hotel when Fawley drove up and entered. He welcomed his returning guest with a beaming smile.

"Monsieur has found the weather inclement, I fear," he remarked.

"Fiendish," was the emphatic reply. "No more of your mountains for me, Monsieur Carlotti. I have finished with them. Cagnes may be dull golf, but it will be good enough for me."

Carlotti's eyes twinkled with comprehension.

"The telephones have been busy this morning," he observed. "There has been a great deal of disturbance and still is at the frontiers. The weather again without a doubt."

Fawley nodded.

"I shall not trouble the frontiers," he confided. "A few quiet days in this warmth will suit me better."

Carlotti bowed.

"It is good news for us," he declared. "If by chance," he added, as the two men neared the lift, "Monsieur should be in need of a golfing companion there is a Mr. Krust here who would like a game."

"Fix it up for me," Fawley replied. "To-morrow or the next day—as soon as the weather gets decent."

The little man remained below, smiling and bowing. Fawley mounted to his apartments upon the second floor. The valet, whom he met in the corridor, threw open the doors and shutters.

"There have been telephone enquiries for Monsieur," he announced, pointing to some slips upon the table. "No letters."

"A hot bath—quickly," Fawley ordered. "As soon as you have turned the water on find the waiter and order coffee—a large pot—*café complet*."

The valet bustled off. Fawley strolled into the room twenty minutes later in his dressing-gown, a different man. The coffee was steaming upon the table, a delicious fragrance was in the air. He ordered more rolls and butter. In the act of serving himself he stopped abruptly. Upon his writing-table, in a prominent position, was a blue envelope. He called to the valet.

"Henri," he pointed out, "that letter was not on my table when I went to my bath a few minutes ago."

"Certainly it was not, sir."

"Who has been in the room?"

"No one, sir, except the waiter who brought the coffee."

Fawley turned to the latter, who had just reappeared.

"Did you bring that note?" he asked.

The man shook his head.

"*Non, Monsieur*," he replied. "I have not seen it before. Ten minutes ago when I first came it was not there."

Fawley made no further remark. He possessed himself of the note and turned to the valet.

"Send me the coiffeur," he ordered, "in twenty minutes. Afterwards you might put me out a grey tweed suit and flannel shirt."

"No golf or tennis to-day, sir?"

Fawley shook his head. The man disappeared. Fawley poured out the coffee with his right hand. His left palm lay over the letter in the blue envelope. Just at that moment, without any previous warning, there came an almost peremptory knocking at the inside door of the salon.

CHAPTER IX

FAWLEY's left hand conveyed the letter in the blue envelope to the safe recesses of his pocket. His right hand continued its task of pouring out the coffee.

"Come in," he invited.

The door was promptly opened. The person who stood upon the threshold was one of the most harmless-looking elderly gentlemen possible to conceive. He was inclined to be stout, but his broad shoulders and erect carriage somewhat discounted the fact. He was possessed of a pink-and-white complexion, eyes of almost a China-blue and shortly cropped grey hair. He wore a grey knickerbocker suit and carried in his hand a hat of the same colour, of quaint design.

"I have the pleasure to address Major Fawley, is it not so?" he began in a clear, pleasant voice with a slight foreign accent. "I was hoping to present a letter of introduction, but it arrives late. My name is Krust."

"Adolf Krust?" Fawley asked, rising to his feet.

"The same," was the cheerful rejoinder. "You have heard of me, yes?"

"Naturally," Fawley replied. "Anyone who takes an interest in European politics must have heard of Adolf Krust. Come in and sit down, sir."

The visitor shook hands, but hesitated.

"This is not a formal visit," he said. "I ventured to look in to ask if you would care to play golf with me to-day. I have heard of you from a mutual friend, besides this letter of introduction of which I spoke."

"That is quite all right," Fawley assured him. "You have had your coffee, I suppose?"

"At seven o'clock," the other answered. "What I wished to explain was that I am not alone. My two nieces are with me. It is permitted to ask them to enter?"

"By all means," Fawley assented. "I hope they will excuse my rather unconventional attire."

"They are unconventional themselves," Krust declared. "Nina!"

Two young women entered at once. They wore the correct tweed clothes of the feminine golfer, but they rather gave one the impression of being dressed for a scene in a musical comedy. Their bérets were almost too perfect, and the delicacy of their complexions could scarcely have survived a strenuous outdoor life. They were, as a matter of fact, exceedingly pretty girls.

"Let me present Major Fawley," Krust said, waving his hand. "Miss Nina Heldersturm—Miss Greta Müller."

Fawley bowed, shook hands with the young women, apologised for his costume and disposed of them upon a divan.

"We owe you apologies," Krust went on, "for descending upon you like this, but the fact of it is our rooms are all upon this floor. I ventured——"

"Not another word, please," Fawley begged. "I am very glad indeed to meet you, Mr. Krust, and your charming nieces."

"We go to golf," Krust declared. "These young ladies are too frivolous for the pursuit. I myself am a serious golfer. It has been said of me that I take my nieces with me to distract my opponents!"

"We never say a word," one of the young ladies protested.

"We really have very good golf manners," the other put in. "If we are allowed to walk round we never speak upon the stroke, we never stand in anyone's line, and we always say 'hard luck' when anyone misses a putt."

"You have been well trained," Fawley approved.

"To serious conversation they are deaf," Krust confided. "They have not a serious thought in their brains. How could it be otherwise? They are Bohemians. Nina there calls herself an artist. She paints passably, but she is lazy. Greta has small parts at the Winter Gardens. Just now we are all in the same position. We are out of harness. Our worthy President has put me temporarily upon the shelf. Nina is waiting for a contract and Greta has no engagements until the summer. We were on our way to Italy—as perhaps you know."

Krust's suddenly wide-opened eyes, his quick lightning-like glance at Fawley, almost took the latter aback.

"I had no idea of the fact," he answered.

"I wish to go to Rome. It was my great desire to arrive there yesterday. A mutual friend of ours, however, said 'No.' A politician cannot travel incognito. My business, it seems, must be done at second hand."

"It is," Fawley ventured, "the penalty of being well known."

Krust stroked his smooth chin. His eyes were still upon Fawley.

"What our friend lacks," he observed, "is audacity. If it is dangerous for me to be in a certain place I call for the photographers and the journalists. I announce my intention of going there. I permit a picture of myself upon the railway platform. What a man is willing to tell to the whole world, the public say, can lead nowhere. One succeeds better in this world by bluff than by subtlety."

"Are you going to play golf with this talkative old gentleman?" Greta asked, smiling at Fawley in heavenly fashion. "We love him, but we are a little tired of him. We should like a change. We should like to walk round with you both, and we promise that our behaviour shall be perfect."

Fawley reflected for a moment. He had the air of a man briefly weighing up the question of an unimportant engagement, but actually his mind had darted backwards to the seventh gallery in the mountains. Step by step he traced his descent. He considered the matter of the changed cars—the ancient Ford lying at the bottom of the precipice, his

Lancia released from its place of hiding in a desolate spot into which he had clambered in the murky twilight after dawn. His change of clothes in a wayside barn. The bundle which lay at the bottom of a river-bed in the valley. Civilian detectives perhaps might have had a chance of tracing that intruder from the hidden galleries, but not military police. If he crossed the frontier now into, say, Switzerland or Germany, he would be weeks ahead of the time and only a trivial part of his task accomplished. The decision which he had intended to take after more leisurely reflection he arrived at now in a matter of seconds.

"If you will wait while I get into some clothes and see my coiffeur, I shall be delighted," he agreed.

Greta flashed at him a little smile of content which left him pondering. Krust picked up his hat and glanced at his watch.

"At eleven o'clock," he pronounced, "we will meet you in the bar below. Rudolf shall mix us an Americano before we start. There is no need for you to bring a car. The thing I have hired here is a perfect omnibus and will take us all."

"Where do we play?" Fawley asked.

"It is a fine morning," the other pointed out. "The glass is going up. The sun is shining. I will telephone to Mont Agel. If play is possible there they will tell me. If not, we will go to Cagnes."

"In the bar at eleven o'clock," Fawley repeated as he showed them out.

Fawley was an absent-minded man that morning. When he submitted himself to the ministrations of the coiffeur and valet his thoughts travelled backwards to his interview with Berati, and travelled forwards exploring the many by-ways of the curious enterprise to which he had committed himself. Krust occupied the principal figure in his reflections. With the papers full of dramatic stories day by day of the political struggle which seemed to be tearing out the heart of a great country, here was one of her principal and most ambitious citizens, with an entourage of frivolity, playing golf on the Riviera. Supposing it were true, as he had hinted, that his presence was due to a desire to visit Berati, why had Berati gone so far as to refuse to see him—a man who might, if chance favoured him, become the ruler of his country? Berati had known of his presence here, had even advised Fawley to cultivate his acquaintance.

"Do you know the gentleman who was in here when you arrived—Monsieur Krust?" he asked his coiffeur abruptly.

The man leaned forward confidentially.

"I shave him every morning, sir," he announced. "A very great German statesman and a millionaire. They say he could have been President if Hindenburg had retired. Everyone is

wondering what he is doing here with things in such a turmoil at home."

"He seems to have good taste in his travelling companions," Fawley observed.

The coiffeur coughed discreetly.

"His nieces, sir. Charming young ladies. Very popular,
too, although the old gentleman seldom lets them out of his
sight. My wife," the man went on, dropping his voice a little,
"was brought up in Germany. She is German, in fact. She
knows the family quite well. She does not seem to remember these young ladies, however."

"I wonder how long he is staying," Fawley meditated.

"Only yesterday morning," the man confided, "he told
me that he was waiting for news from home which might
come at any moment. He is rung up every morning from
Germany. He brought his own private telephone instrument and had it fitted here. He has spoken to Rome once
or twice, too. It is my belief, sir, that he is up to some game
here. From what I can make out by the papers he is just as
well out of Germany while things are in this mess. He has
plenty working for him there."

"Perhaps you are right," Fawley observed indifferently.
"I only read the papers at intervals, but it seemed to me that
he had a party there, and to be rather an odd thing for him
to be so far away with the elections coming on.... Just a snip

on the left hand side, Ernest," Fawley went on, glancing into the mirror.

"The usual time to-night, sir?" the man asked, stepping back to observe his handiwork.

His customer nodded. For several moments after the coiffeur had left him he remained in his chair glancing into the mirror. He was utterly free from vanity and his inspection of himself was purely impersonal. Something to thank his ancestry for, he reflected. No one, to look at him, would believe for a moment the story of his last night's adventures, would believe that he had been for hours in peril of his life, in danger of a chance bullet, in danger of his back to a wall and a dozen bullets concerning which there would be no chance whatever, in danger of broken limbs or a broken neck, committing his body to the perils of the gorges and precipices with only a few feet between him and eternity. There were lines upon his healthy, slightly sunburnt face with its firmly chiselled features and bright hard eyes, but they were the lines of experiences which had failed to age. They were the lines turning slightly upwards from his mouth, the fainter ones at the corners of his eyes, the single furrow across his forehead. Life and his forebears had been kind to him. If he failed in this—the greatest enterprise of his life—it would not be his health or his nerve that would play him false. The turn of the wheel against him might do it.... Below him the people were streaming into the Casino.

He smiled thoughtfully as he reflected that amongst these worshippers of the world-powerful false goddess he was the one man of whom a famous American diplomat, praising his work, had declared—Fawley never leaves anything to chance.

The valet put his head in at the door.

"Your bath is ready, sir," he announced respectfully.

CHAPTER X

SEVERAL minor surprises were in store for Fawley that morning. On the first tee, having to confess to a handicap of two at St. Andrews, and Krust speaking of a nebulous twenty, he offered his opponent a stroke a hole, which was enthusiastically accepted. Fawley, who had an easy and graceful swing, cut his first drive slightly, but still lay two hundred yards down the course a little to the left-hand side. Krust, wielding a driver with an enormous head, took up the most extraordinary posture. He stood with both feet planted upon the ground and he moved on to his toes and back on to his heels once or twice as though to be sure that his stance was rigid. After that he drew the club head back like lightning, lifted it barely past his waist and, without moving either foot from the ground in the slightest degree and with only the smallest attempt at a pivot, drove the ball steadily down the course to within twenty yards of Fawley's. The latter tried to resist a smile.

"Does Mr. Krust do that every time?" he asked Greta, who had attached herself to his side.

She nodded.

"And you need not smile about it," she enjoined. "You wait till the eighteenth green."

For eleven holes Krust played the golf of an automatic but clumsy machine. Only once did he lift his left heel from the ground and then he almost missed the ball altogether. The rest of the time he played every shot, transforming himself into a steady and immovable pillar and simply supplying all the force necessary with his arms and wrists. At the eleventh Fawley, who was two down, paused to look at the view. They all stood on the raised tee and gazed eastwards. The sting from the snow-capped mountains gave just that peculiar tang to the air which seems to supply the alcohol of life. Facing them was a point where the mountains dropped to the sea and the hillside towns and villages boasted their shelf of pasture land above the fertile valleys. Fawley turned towards the north. It was like a dream to remember that less than eleven hours ago he was committing his body to the mercies of those seemingly endless slopes, clutching at tree stumps, partially embedded rocks, clawing even at the ground to brake his progress.

"The frontier over that way," Krust remarked cheerfully.

"What? Into Italy?" Greta demanded.

"Into Italy," Fawley replied. "A strange but not altogether barbarous country. Have you ever visited it?"

She indulged in a little grimace.

"Don't try to be superior, please," she begged. "Americans and English people are always like that. I studied in Milan for two years."

"I was only chaffing, of course," Fawley apologised.

"And I," Nina confided, tugging at Krust's arm, "have worked in Florence. This dear uncle of mine sent me there."

A warning shout from behind sent them on to the tee. In due course the match was finished and Fawley tasted the sweets of defeat.

"I think," he told his companion good-humouredly, "that you are the most remarkable golfer I have ever seen."

Krust smiled all over his face.

"With a figure like mine," he demanded, "what would you do? I have watched others. I have seen how little the body counts for. Only the arms and wrists. I turn my body into a monument. I never move my head or my feet. If I do I fail. It is an idea—yes? All the same it is not a great amusement. I get stiff with the monotony of playing. I miss the exercise of twisting my body. Now, you pay me the price of a ball and I stand drinks for everybody and lunch to follow."

"The loser pays for lunch," Fawley declared cheerfully. "I accept the cocktails, warning you that I am going to drink two."

"And I also," Greta remarked. "I must console myself for my partner's defeat!"

Luncheon was a pleasant meal. They sat in the bald, undecorated restaurant with its high windows, out of which they seemed in incredibly close touch with the glorious panorama of snow-capped hills rolling away to the mists.

"There is no worse golf course in the world," Krust declared enthusiastically, "but there is none set in more beautiful surroundings. My heart is heavy these days, but the air here makes me feel like a boy. I make of life a fail-ure—I come here with the disappointed cry of the people I love in my ears and I can forget."

"We help," Nina pleaded softly, laying her hand upon his sleeve.

"Yes, you help," he admitted, with a curiously clouded look in his blue eyes. "Youth can always help middle age. Still, it remains a terrible thing for a man of action to remain idle. Would it break your hearts, my two little beams of sunshine, if we packed our trunks and sailed away north-wards?"

"It would break mine," Greta declared, touching Fawley's hand as though by accident.

"And mine," Nina echoed.

That was the last of serious conversation until they descended, some short time after luncheon, into the Princi-pality. In the hall of the hotel Fawley handed his golf clubs to the porter and took his leave somewhat abruptly. He had scarcely reached his room, however, before there was a knock at the door. Krust entered. Fawley welcomed him a little grudgingly.

"Sorry if I hurried away," he apologised, "but I really have work to do."

"Five minutes," Krust begged. "I understand something of your profession, Major Fawley. I passed some time in our own Foreign Office. For the moment, though, it happens that I must disregard it. I have not the temperament that brooks too long delay. Answer me, please. Our friend in Rome spoke to you of my presence here? Did he give you any message, any word as to his decision?"

"None whatever," Fawley replied cautiously. "To tell you the truth, I don't know what you are talking about."

A flaming light shone for a moment in the cold blue eyes.

"That is Berati—the Italian of him—the oversubtlety! The world is ours if he will make up his mind, and he hesitates between me—who have more real power in Germany than any other man—and one who must be nameless even between us, but to whom if he leaned our whole great scheme would go 'pop' like an exploded shell. Were you to make reports upon me? To give an opinion of my capacity?"

"I had other work to do here," Fawley said calmly. "I was simply told to cultivate your acquaintance. The rest I thought would come later."

"It may come too late," Krust declared. "Berati cannot trifle and twiddle his thumbs for ever. Listen, Major Fawley. How much do you know of what is on the carpet?"

"Something," Fawley admitted. "Broad ideas. That's all. No details. Nothing certain. I am working from hand to mouth."

"Listen," Krust insisted. "There is a scheme. It was Berati's, I admit that, although it came perhaps from a brain greater than his—someone who stands in the shadows behind him. It called for a swift alliance between Germany and Italy. An Anglo-Saxon neutrality. Swift action. Africa for Italy. A non-military Germany, but a Germany which would soon easily rule the world. And when the moment comes to strike, Berati is hesitating! He hesitates only with whom to deal in Germany. He dares to hesitate between one who has the confidence of the whole German nation and a man who has been cast aside like a pricked bladder, whose late adherents are swarming into my camp, and the man whose name, were it once pronounced, would be the ruin of our scheme. And he cannot decide! I have had enough. I am forbidden to approach Berati—courteously, firmly. Very well. By to-morrow morning I come back to you with the truth."

Fawley was mystified. He knew very well that his companion was moved by a rare passion, but exactly what had provoked it was hard to tell.

"Look here, Herr Krust——" he began.

It was useless. The man seemed to have lost control of himself. He stamped up and down the room. He passed through the inner and the outer doors leading into the corridor. A few moments later Fawley, from his balcony, saw the huge car in which they had driven up to Mont Agel circle round by the Casino and turn northwards.... Fawley, with a constitution as nearly as possible perfect for his thirty-seven years, felt a sense of not altogether unpleasant weariness as he turned away from the window. His night of strenuous endeavour, physical and mental, his golf that morning in the marvellous atmosphere of Mont Agel, had their effect. He was suddenly weary. He discarded his golf clothes, took a shower, put on an old smoking-suit and threw himself upon the bed. In five minutes he was asleep. When he awoke the sunshine had changed to twilight, a twilight that was almost darkness. He glanced at his watch. It was seven o'clock. He had slept for three hours and a half. He swung himself off the bed and suddenly paused to listen. There was a light through the chink of the door leading into his salon. He listened again for a moment, then he opened the first door softly and tried the handle of the second only to find it locked against him. Someone was in his salon surreptitiously, someone who had dared to turn his own key against him! His first impulse was to smile at the ingenuousness of such a proceeding. He thrust on a dressing-gown, took a small automatic from one of the drawers of his bureau, stole out into the corridor and knocked at the door of the sitting-room. For a moment or two there was silence. Whoever was inside had evidently not taken the trouble to prepare against outside callers. A sound like the crumpling of paper had ceased. The light went out and was then turned on again. The door was opened. Greta stood there utterly taken by surprise.

"A flank movement," he remarked coolly, closing the door behind him. "Now, young lady, please tell me what you are doing in my sitting-room and why you locked the door against me."

She was speechless for a moment. Fawley crossed the room and stood on the other side of the table behind which she had retreated. His eyes travelled swiftly round the apartment. A large despatch box of formidable appearance had been disturbed but not apparently opened. One of the drawers of his writing desk had been pulled out.

"Is this an effort on your own behalf, Miss Greta?" he continued, "or are you trying to give your uncle a little assistance?"

"You are not very nice to me," she complained pathetically. "Are you not pleased to find me here?"

"Well," he answered, "that depends."

She threw herself into an easy chair.

"Are you angry that I have ventured to pay you a visit?" she persisted.

He sighed.

"If only the visit were to me! On the other hand, I find myself locked out of my own salon."

"Locked out," she repeated wonderingly. "Just what do you mean? So far from locking you out I was wondering whether I dared come and disturb you."

He moved across towards the double doors and opened them without difficulty.

"H'm, that's odd," he observed, looking round at her quickly. "I tried this inner door just now. It seemed to me to be locked."

"I, too—I found it stiff," she said. "I first thought that you had locked yourself in, then I found that it gave quite easily if one turned the right way."

"You have been into my bedroom?"

She smiled up into his face.

"Do you mind? My uncle has gone away—no one knows where. Nina has gone motoring with a friend to Nice. I am left alone. I do not like being by myself. I come along here, I knock softly at the door of your sitting-room. No reply. I enter. Emptiness. I think I will see if you are sleeping. I open both those doors without any particular difficulty. I see you lying on the bed. I go softly over. You sleep—oh, how you were sleeping!"

Her eyes met Fawley's without flinching. There stole into his brain a faint recollection that some time during that deep slumber of his there had come to him a dreamlike suggestion of a perfume which had reminded him of the girl, a faint consciousness, not strong enough to wake him, of the presence of something agreeable. She was probably telling him the truth.

"I had not the heart to wake you," she went on. "I stole out again. I sat in your easy-chair and I waited."

"I perceive," he pointed out, "that a drawer of my writing-table is open and that my despatch-box has changed its position."

Her eyes opened a little wider.

"You do not think that I am a thief?"

"How can I tell? Why did you open that drawer?"

"To find some notepaper. I thought that I would write some letters."

"Why did you move my despatch-box?"

"For the same purpose," she assured him. "I found it locked, so I left it alone. Do you think that I came to steal something? Can you not believe that I came because I was lonely—to see you?"

He smiled.

"To tell you the truth," he admitted, "I cannot see what else you could have come for. I have no secrets from Mr. Krust."

"But you have," she exclaimed impetuously. "You will not tell him what he so much wants to know."

"So that is why you are here," Fawley remarked with a faint smile. "You want to see if you can find out for your uncle Berati's disposition towards him, and you think that I may have papers. My little butterfly lady, you are very much an amateur at this sort of thing, aren't you? Men do not carry papers nowadays. It is too dangerous. Besides, who am I to see what lies behind Berati's mind?"

"I tell you that I care nothing about Berati," she cried suddenly. "I was weary of being alone and I came to see you."

She moved across and stood beside him. She was wearing some sort of negligee between golf and dinner costume, something in one piece with vivid flashes of scarlet and wide sleeves, and her arm rested affectionately upon his shoulders.

"Please do not be horrid to me," she begged. "Mr. Krust has been very kind to me. If we could help him—either Nina or I—we should do so, but not at your expense."

"You would have no chance, little Greta," he told her with a very gentle caress. "Since we seem to be arriving at an understanding, tell me what I can do for you."

"First of all," she said, drawing her arm tighter around him, "try to believe that I am not the frivolous little idiot I sometimes try to appear. Secondly, believe also that when I came here this afternoon the great thing in my mind was to see you, not to be like one of the adventuresses of fiction and pry about for papers; and thirdly, as I am left all alone, I thought perhaps you might take pity on me and ask me to dine—just you and I alone—only much later."

He looked out of the window, over which the curtains had not yet been drawn, at the flashing lamps of the square and farther away at the lights stealing out from the black curtain of the shrouded hillside.

"My dear," he protested, "you are inviting me to flirt with you."

"Is it so difficult?" she whispered. "I am much nicer than you think I am. I am much fonder of you than you could believe."

"It would not be difficult at all," he assured her. "But alas! how would you feel when I told you, as I would have to very soon, that most of the time when I am not thinking of more serious things I spend thinking of another woman?"

She stood quite still and he had a queer fancy that the soft palm which she had stretched out upon his cheek grew colder. It was several moments before she spoke.

"I would be sorry," she confessed. "But, after all, the days are past when a man thinks only of one woman. It was beautiful to read of and think of, but one scarcely hopes for it now. Who is she, please?"

"What does it matter?" he answered. "I am not sure that I trust her any more than I trust you. The truth of it is I am a clumsy fellow with women. I have lived so long with the necessity of trusting no one that I cannot get out of the habit of it."

She hesitated for a moment.

"I can be truthful," she said earnestly. "With you I would like to be. It was not writing-paper I searched for in your drawer, and if I could have opened your box I should have done so. I have a bunch of keys in my pocket."

"But what is it you are hoping to find?" he asked.

"Mr. Krust," she said, "thinks that you must know towards which party in Germany Berati is leaning. He thinks that you must know the reason why he is not allowed to go to Rome."

"Supposing I assured you," he told her, "that I have not the faintest idea what lies behind Berati's mind. He has not asked my advice nor given me his opinion. I have learnt more from Mr. Krust than from him. I have not a single paper in my possession which would interest you in any way. If I might make a wild guess, it would be that Berati is afraid that Krust might gain access to and influence the greater man who stands behind him."

"Is that the truth?" she asked fervently.

"It is the honest truth," he assured her. "You see, therefore, that I am useless so far as regards your schemes. Realising that, if you would like to dine with me I should be delighted."

"If you want me to," she consented eagerly. "I believe you think that I am very terrible. Perhaps I am, but not in the way you imagine. Do you want me to dine with you, Major Fawley? Would it give you pleasure?"

"Of course it would," he answered. "I warn you that I am a very wooden sort of person, but I am all alone for to-night at any rate, and you are not an unattractive young woman, are you?"

She smiled a little oddly.

"Well, I do not know," she said. "I do not think that unless a clever man has a flair for women we girls have much to offer. What time, please?"

"Nine o'clock," he decided. "You shall tell me about Germany and the life there. I am rather curious. I find the political parties almost impossible to understand. You may make a disciple of me!"

"Perhaps," she murmured, as she took her very reluctant leave, "we might find something even more interesting to talk about than German politics."

CHAPTER XI

FAWLEY felt that fate treated him scurvily that evening. Some great European notable staying in the Hôtel de France had taken it into his head to entertain the local Royalty, who seldom if ever was seen in public, and Greta and he had scarcely established themselves at their corner table before, amidst a buzz of interest, a very distinguished company of guests made their way towards the magnificently beflowered and ornamented table which had been reserved for them. There were Princes and Princesses in the gathering, Dukes and Duchesses, men and women of note in every walk of life, and—Elida. She came towards the end of the procession, walking side by side with a famous English diplomat, and she passed within a yard or two of Fawley's table. For the moment he was taken unawares. He half rose to his feet, his eyes even sought hers, but in vain. If she was surprised at seeing him there and under such circumstances she gave no sign. She passed on without a break in her conversation, easily the most distinguished-looking figure of the party, in her plain black frock and her famous pearls.

"What a beautiful woman," Greta sighed, "and I believe that you know her."

Fawley, who had recovered from his momentary aberration, smiled.

"Yes," he admitted, "once upon a time I knew her—slightly."

"What will she think of you?" Greta reflected. "I wonder how long it is since you have met. Will she think that you have married or that, like everyone else who comes to this quaint corner of the world, you have brought with you your favourite companion?"

"She probably won't think of me at all," Fawley replied. "We only met for one day and ours was rather a stormy acquaintance, as a matter of fact."

"She is more beautiful than I am," Greta confessed naïvely. "She looks very cold, though. I am not cold. I have too much heart. I think that is the pity about Germans. We are abused all over the world, I know, but we are too sentimental."

"Sentimentality is supposed to be one of your national characteristics," Fawley observed, "but I do not think your menkind at any rate allow it to stand in the way of business—of their progress in life, perhaps I should say."

"Adolf Krust is sentimental," she continued, "but with him all his feelings seem to be centred on his country. He loves women, but they mean little to him. He is what I call a passionate patriot. At any cost, anyhow, he wants to see Germany stand where she did amongst the nations."

"Almost the same with you, isn't it?"

She shook her head.

"Not quite. Very few women in the world have ever put love of country before love of their lover. I suppose we are too selfish. I am fond of Germany, although I see her faults, but she could not possibly occupy all my affections."

"You are rather intriguing, aren't you?" he remarked. "I should like to know you better."

"Ask me questions, then," she suggested.

"How old are you?"

"Twenty-two."

"Where were you educated?"

"In London, Paris, Dresden, a short time for my voice in Milan. I may be anything you like to fancy, but I have never known poverty."

"And Krust—he is really your uncle?"

She hesitated.

"We are rather on delicate ground," she remarked, "because Nina is in this, of course. No, he is not our uncle. Nina and I have both developed a passion for politics. Nina worked for some time in a public office without salary. It was through her that I became interested. Now I honestly believe politics—we use the word in Germany in a broader sense than you do—have become the great interest of my life. I want Krust to be Chancellor and, more still, I want him, when the proper time comes, to decide how Germany shall be governed."

"What about the President?"

"A stupid office. One man is enough to rule any country. If he fails, he should be either shot or deposed. Adolf Krust is the only man whom the great mass of Germans would trust. What we need in Central Europe is a shock. People would make up their minds then quickly. At present we are drifting. That is why Krust, who hates to leave his work for a moment, who hates games and the sunshine of foreign places and gambling and all recreations, has come down here to be nearer to the one man who seems to hold the fate of Europe in his hand just now. He will be disappointed. I feel that. His rival has powerful agents at work in Italy."

"I am a little confused about German affairs," Fawley confessed. "Who is his rival?"

She glanced at him for permission and lit a cigarette. Their dinner had been well chosen and excellently served, but she had eaten sparingly. She took a long draught of champagne, however.

"Heinrich Behrling."

"The communist?" Fawley exclaimed.

She shook her head.

"Behrling is no communist. He is not even a socialist. He is the apostle of the new Fascism."

"Krust, then?"

"If I am telling you secrets," she said, "I shall be very ashamed of myself. I do not think, though, that Adolf Krust would mind. He has tried to make a confidant of you. Krust is for the re-establishment of the monarchy."

"Heavens!" Fawley murmured. "I thought that General von Salzenburg was the head of the aristocratic party."

"So does he," she replied simply. "This is our trouble, you see. We are not united. Come to Berlin and you may find out. Why do you not get Berati to give you a freer hand? Then I think that we could convince you."

"But, my dear child," Fawley protested, "I am nothing to General Berati. I am just an agent who was out of work whom he has trusted to make a few observations. I have never even met his chief. I am a subordinate without any particular influence."

She shook her head.

"You may deceive yourself, or you may think it well to deceive me," she said. "Adolf Krust would never believe it."

"By the by," Fawley asked, "where has your reputed uncle hurried off to?"

"You tell me so little and you expect me to tell you everything," she complained. "He has gone to San Remo to telephone to Berati. If Berati permits it, he will go on to Rome—that is what he is so anxious to do. To go there and not be received, however, would ruin his cause. The other side would proclaim it as a great triumph. Von Salzenburg, too, would be pleased."

"You seem to have a very fair grasp of events," Fawley remarked, as they entered upon the last course of their dinner. "Tell me, do you believe in this impending war?"

Again she showed signs of impatience. She frowned and there was a distinct pout upon her full but beautifully shaped lips.

"Always the same," she exclaimed. "You ask questions, you tell nothing, and yet you know. You take advantage of the poor little German girl because she is sentimental and because she likes you. Ask me how much I care and I will tell you. What should I know about wars? Ask a soldier. Ask them at the Quai d'Orsay. Ask them at Whitehall in London. Or ask Berati."

"These people would probably tell me to mind my own business," Fawley declared.

Her eyes twinkled.

"It is a very good answer."...

They had coffee in Fawley's salon—an idea of Greta's. She wanted to be near if Adolf Krust should return in despair. But time passed on and there was no sign of Krust. They sat in easy-chairs watching the lights in the gardens and listening to the music from across the way. They sat in the twilight that they might see Krust's car more easily should it put in an appearance. Conversation grew more spasmodic. Fawley, he scarcely knew why, was suddenly tired of speculations.

The great world over the mountains was moving on to a crisis, that he knew well enough, but his brain was weary. He wondered dimly whether for the last few years he had not taken life too seriously. Would any other man have felt the fatigue he was feeling? He half turned his head. The outline of the girl in her blue satin frock was only just visible. The vague light from outside was shimmering in her hair. Her eyes were seeking for his, a little distended, as though behind their sweetness there lay something of anxious doubt. The swift rise and fall of her slim bosoms, the icy coldness of her hand resting lightly in his, seemed to indicate something of the same emotion. Her fingers suddenly gripped his passionately.

"Why are you so difficult?" she asked. "You do not like me, perhaps?"

"On the contrary," he assured her, "I like you very much. I find you very attractive but far too distracting."

"How distracting?" she demanded.

"Because, as we all know—you and I and the others," he went on—"love-making is not part of our present scheme of life. It might complicate it. It would not help."

"All the time you reason," she complained. "It is not much that I ask. I make no vows. I ask for none. I should like very much, as we say in Germany, to walk hand in hand with you a little way in life."

"To share my life," he reflected, "my thoughts, and my work—yes?"

There was a tinge of colour in her cheeks.

"Leave off thinking," she cried almost passionately. "Many men have lost the sweetest things in life through being choked with suspicions. Cannot you——"

There was commotion outside. The opening of a door, heavy footsteps, a thundering knocking at the inner door flung open almost immediately. Krust entered out of breath, his clothes disarranged with travel, yet with something of triumph dancing in his blue eyes. He was carrying his heavy spectacles, he flung his hat upon the table and struggled with his coat.

"My friend," he exclaimed, "and little Greta! Good. I wanted to speak to you both. Listen. I have talked with Berati."

"You are to go to Rome?" Fawley demanded.

"I have abandoned the idea," Krust declared. "For the moment it is not necessary. There is another thing more important. I say to Berati—'Give me a trusted agent, let him visit the places I shall mark down, let him leave with me for three days in Berlin, and then let him report to you. No rubbish from inspired newspapers with Jew millionaires behind them. The truth! It is there to be seen. Give me the chance of showing it.' I spoke of you, Fawley, indefinitely, but Berati understood. Oh, he is swift to understand, that man. To-morrow you will have your word. To-morrow night you will leave for Germany. I ask pardon—for half an hour I spoke on the private wire at the Royal Hotel in San Remo. From there I jumped into the car and we have driven—I can tell you that we have driven! You excuse?"

A waiter had entered the room with two bottles of beer in ice-pails and a large tumbler. Krust filled it to the brim, threw back his head and drank. He set down the glass empty.

"It is good news which I bring?" he asked Fawley anxiously. "You are satisfied to come?"

Fawley's eyes travelled for a moment to the dark line of mountains beyond Roquefort. There had been rumours that the French were combing the whole Principality watching for a spy. Monsieur Carlotti had spoken of it lightly enough, but with some uneasiness. Fawley tapped a cigarette upon the table and lit it.

"A visit to Germany just now," he admitted, "should be interesting."

Krust in his own salon an hour later looked curiously across the room to where Greta was standing, an immovable figure, at the open window. He had rested and eaten since his journey, but there were unusual lines in his smooth face and his expression of universal benevolence had disappeared. Greta half turned her head. Her tone was almost sullen.

"You had success with our impenetrable friend?" Krust asked.

"I did my best," she replied. "You came back too soon."

CHAPTER XII

ON his way down to the quay the next morning Fawley read again the note which had been brought to him with his morning coffee. It was written on the Hôtel de France notepaper, but there was no formal commencement or ending.

> *"I am very anxious to talk to you privately, but not in the hotel, where you seem to have become surrounded by an entourage which I mistrust. One of my friends has a small yacht here—the 'Sea Hawk'—lying on the western side of the harbour. Will you come down and see me there at half-past eleven this morning? It is very, very important, so do not fail me.*
>
> *"E."*

The horse's hoofs clattered noisily on the cobbled road fringing the dock. Fawley slowly returned the letter to his pocket. It seemed reasonable enough. The *Sea Hawk* was there all right—a fine-looking schooner yacht flying the pennant of an international club and the German national flag. Fawley paid the *cocher* and dismissed him, walked down the handsome gangway and received the salute of a heavily built but smartly turned-out officer.

"It is the gentleman whom Madame la Princesse is expecting?" the man enquired, with a strong German accent. "If the gnädiger Herr will come this way."

Fawley followed the man along the deck to the companionway, descended a short flight of stairs and was ushered into a large and comfortable cabin fitted up as a sitting-room.

"I will fetch the Princess," his guide announced. "The gentleman will be so kind as to repose himself and wait."

Fawley subsided into an easy-chair and took up a magazine. In the act of turning over the pages, however, he paused suddenly. For a moment he listened. Then he rose to his feet and, crossing the room swiftly, tried the handle of the door. His hearing, which was always remarkably good, had not deceived him. The door was locked! Fawley stood back and whistled softly under his breath. The affair presented itself to him as a magnificent joke. It was rather like Elida, he decided, with her queer, dramatic gestures. He pressed the bell. There was no response. Suddenly a familiar sound startled him—the anchors being drawn up. The Diesel engines were already beating rhythmically. A moment or two later they were moving. The grimmer lines in his face relaxed. A smile flickered at the corners of his lips.

"Abducted," he murmured.

He looked out of the porthole and gazed at the idlers on the quay from which they were gliding away. There was a pause, a churning of the sea and a swing round. The *Sea Hawk* was evidently for a cruise. She passed out of the harbour and her course was set seawards. Fawley lit a cigarette and took up a magazine. It appeared to him that this was a time for inaction. He decided to let events develop. In due course what he had expected happened—there was a knock at the door of the very luxurious and beautifully decorated green and gold cabin in which he was confined. Fawley laid down his magazine and listened. The knock was repeated—a pompous, peremptory sound, the summons of the conqueror in some mimic battle determined to abide by the grim courtesies of warfare.

"Come in!" Fawley invited.

There was the sound of a key being turned. The door was opened. A tall, broad-shouldered man with sunburnt cheeks and a small closely cropped yellow moustache presented himself. He was apparently of youthful middle age, he wore the inevitable mufti of the sea—blue serge, double-breasted jacket, grey flannel trousers and white shoes. He had the bearing of an aristocrat discounted by a certain military arrogance.

"Major Fawley, I believe?" he enquired.

"You have the advantage of me, sir," was the cool reply.

"My name is Prince Maurice von Thal," the new-comer announced. "I have come for a friendly talk."

"Up till now," Fawley observed, "the element of friendliness seems to have been lacking in your reception of me. Nevertheless," he added, "I should be glad to hear what you have to say."

"Monte Carlo just now is a little overcrowded. You understand me, I dare say."

"I can guess," Fawley replied. "But who are you? I came to visit the Princess Elida di Vasena."

"The Princess is on board. She is associated with me in our present enterprise."

Fawley nodded.

"Of course," he murmured. "I knew that I had seen you somewhere before. You were in the party who were entertaining the local Royalties last night at the Hôtel de France."

"That is so."

Fawley glanced out of the porthole. They were heading for the open seas now and travelling at a great speed. On the right was the Rock with its strangely designed medley of buildings. The flag was flying from the Palace and the Cathedral bell was ringing.

"Many things have happened to me in life," he reflected with a smile, "but I have never before been kidnapped."

"It sounds a little like musical comedy, doesn't it?" the Prince remarked. "The fact is—it was my cousin's idea. She was anxious to talk to you, but the hotel is full of spies and she could think of no safe place in the neighbourhood."

"I thought there was something fishy about that note," Fawley sighed. "Is Princess Elida really on board?"

"She certainly is," was the prompt reply. "Wait one moment. I will summon her. I can assure you that she is impatient to meet you again."

He stepped back to the doorway and called out her name. There came the sound of light footsteps descending from the deck. Elida, in severe but very delightful yachting attire, entered the room. She nodded pleasantly to Fawley.

"I hope Maurice has apologised and all that sort of thing," she said. "We had no intention of really keeping you here by force, of course, but it did occur to us that you might not want to be seen in discussion with us by your other friends here."

"It might have been awkward," Fawley admitted pleasantly. "It is humiliating, though, to be whisked off like this. Your designs might have been far more sinister and then I should have felt very much like the booby who walked into the trap. There is nothing I enjoy so much as a cruise. Wouldn't it be pleasanter on deck, though?"

"As you please," the Prince assented. "There is a little movement, but that is not likely to hurt any of us. As a matter of form, Major, may I beg for your word of honour that you will not seek to call the attention of any passing craft to your presence here?"

"I give it with pleasure," was the prompt acquiescence.

They found a sheltered divan on the port side of the boat. A white-coated steward arranged a small table and appeared presently with a cocktail shaker and champagne in an ice-pail. The Prince drank the latter out of a tumbler. Elida and Fawley preferred cocktails. Caviare sandwiches were served and cigarettes.

"This is very agreeable," Fawley declared. "May I ask how far we are going?"

The Prince sighed.

"Alas, it can be only a short cruise," he regretted. "The Princess is unfortunately commanded to lunch."

"Then I suggest," Fawley said, "that we commence our conversation."

Elida leaned forward. She looked earnestly at her opposite neighbour.

"We want to know, Major Fawley, whether it is true that you are going to Germany with Adolf Krust and his two decoys?"

"We should also," the Prince added, "like to know with what object you are visiting that country and whether you are going as the accredited agent of Berati?"

"Would it not be simpler for you to ask General Berati?" Fawley suggested.

"You know quite well," Elida reminded him, "that for the present I am not allowed in Italy. Believe me, if I were there I should find out; but I may not go, and I know well that my letters here are tampered with. Prince Patoni promised me news, but nothing has come."

Fawley reflected for a moment.

"How did you know," he asked, "that I was going to Germany?"

She smiled.

"My dear man," she protested, "I am, after all, in a small way doing your sort of work. I must have a few—what is it you say in English?—irons in the fire. Adolf Krust, I hear, is hoping for great things from the little girl. Are you susceptible, I wonder?"

Fawley looked steadily across at the Princess.

"I never thought so until about a month ago," he answered. "Since then I have wondered."

She sighed.

"Perhaps if my hair were that wonderful colour and my morals as elastic, do you think I could throw a yoke of roses around your neck and lead you into Germany myself?"

"A pathetic figure," Fawley observed. "I will go with you to Germany at any time you invite me, Princess. But I should carry out my work when I got there in exactly the way I intend to now."

"I want you to meet General von Salzenburg," she murmured.

"The world's fire-eater," Fawley remarked.

"These damned newspapers!" Von Thal exclaimed angrily in his deep bass voice. "What is it to be a fire-eater? Fire purges the earth. God knows Europe needs it!"

"I am not a pacifist by any means," Fawley protested, accepting a cigarette from Elida. "In the old days war was the logical method of settling disputes. There was no question of reparation. The victorious nation cut off a chunk of the other's country and everything went on merrily afterwards. Those days have gone. War does not fit in with a civilisation the basis of which is economic."

Von Thal stiffened visibly. One could almost feel the muscles swelling underneath his coat.

"It seems strange to hear an ex-army man, as I presume you are, Major Fawley, talking in such a fashion," he declared. "To us war is a holy thing. It is a means of redemption. It is a great purifier. We shall not agree very well, Major Fawley, if you are going to tell us that you are a convert of Krust's."

"I am not going to tell you anything of the sort," Fawley replied, helping himself to another sandwich. "As a matter of fact, I have had very little conversation with Herr Krust. Between our three selves, as the Princess here has had proof of it, I am working on behalf of Italy. All I have to do is to make a report of the political situation in Germany as I conceive it. The rest remains with General Berati and his master. Besides," he went on, "it would be very foolish to imagine that my reports would be more than a drop in the bucket of information which Berati is accumulating. He is a very sage and far-seeing man and he is collecting the points of view of as many people as he can."

Von Thal grunted.

"I am afraid," he pronounced, "that our conversation is not approaching a satisfactory termination."

"You see," Elida murmured softly, "our information does not exactly coincide with what you tell us. We believe that Berati is prepared to shape his policy according to your report. The great national patriotic party of Germany, to which my cousin here and I belong, and of which General von Salzenburg is the titular chief, is the only party which we believe in, and for our success we must have the sympathy of and the alliance with Italy."

"And war?" Fawley queried gravely.

"Why should I deny it?" she answered. "And war. You do not know perhaps how well prepared Germany is for war. I doubt whether even Adolf Krust knows, but we know. War alone will free Germany from her fetters. This time it will not be a war of doubtful results. Everything is pre-arranged. Success is certain. Italy will have what she covets—Africa. Germany will be once more mistress of Europe."

"Very interesting," Fawley conceded. "You may possibly be right. When I get back from Germany I shall very likely be in a position to tell you so. At present I have an open mind."

Von Thal poured himself out a glass of wine and drank it. He turned to Elida. His expression was unpleasant.

"This conversation," he said, "has reached an unsatisfactory point. The Princess and I must confer. Will you come below with me, Elida?"

She shook her head slowly.

"For what purpose, dear cousin? We cannot stretch this obstinate gentleman upon the rack until he changes his mind."

"Neither," Von Thal said savagely, "can we turn him loose to hob-nob with Krust to destroy the golden chance of this century. It must be Von Salzenburg who signs the treaty with Italy—never Adolf Krust or any other man."

"That," Fawley observed quietly, "is not for us to decide."

Von Thal, a mighty figure of a man, took a quick step forward. Elida's arm shot out, her fingers pressed against the lapels of his coat.

"There is nothing to be done in this fashion, Maurice," she insisted. "Major Fawley is our guest."

"It is not true," Von Thal declared. "He is our prisoner. I, for one, do not believe in his neutrality. I believe that he is committed to Krust. He is for the bourgeoisie. This is not a private quarrel, Elida. It is not a private affair of honour. We must do our duty to the party for whom we work, for the cause which we have made ours."

"It seems to me a most unpleasant way of ending a mild argument, this," Fawley ventured. "I told you that I have given no pledges. My mind is not made up. It will not be made up until I have visited Germany. I have accepted your invitation to discuss the matter. You are displeased with me. What is there to be done about it? You are not, I presume, thinking of murder."

"To kill a man who is an enemy to one's country is not murder," Von Thal shouted.

"To kill a guest," Fawley retorted, "is against the conventions even amongst savages!"

"You are not a guest," Von Thal denied. "You are the prisoner who walked into a trap. That is a part of warfare. It seems to me you are to be treated as a man enemy."

"Have it your own way," Fawley yielded. "Anyway, those are the best caviare sandwiches I ever ate in my life."

Elida laughed softly. She laid her hand upon Von Thal's arm.

"Maurice," she pleaded, "yours is a hopeless attitude. Major Fawley is too distinguished a personage to be treated without due consideration, and I, for one, have no wish to see the inside of a French prison."

"What am I here for then?" Von Thal demanded angrily. "I prefer deeds to words."

"So do the most foolish of us," Elida murmured. "But the way must be prepared. We cannot frighten Major Fawley as we might a weaker man."

"Our country is worth lying for," Von Thal declared. "Why should we not report that Fawley, taking a short cruise with us, slipped and fell overboard? No one can say otherwise."

"Major Fawley," Elida objected disdainfully, "is not one of those men who slip on decks, especially with rails like we have and in a calm sea. Be reasonable, Maurice."

"I am for plain actions and plain words," Von Thal persisted. "You tell me that you have information that Berati has placed his faith in this man. He is sending him to Germany to report upon the situation, to choose between Krust, Behrling and us, in plain words. Very well. You go on to say that you fear he will decide for Krust."

"I did not go so far as that," Elida protested earnestly. "Only yesterday Berati refused to receive Krust. He had to come back from San Remo, where he went to telephone. He refused to see him or to take him anywhere else for an audience. The matter is not decided. Our object with Major Fawley should be to get him to promise that we have fair play, that he shall see something of our organisations and hear something of our plans as well as Krust's. After that will come the time for arguments, and after that, Maurice, but not before, might come the time for the sort of action you are contemplating."

She was suddenly more grave. There was a smouldering light in her eyes. She turned to face Fawley.

"If we arrive at that stage," she said, "and we are faced with an unfavourable decision, I think I would send the dearest friend or the dearest relative I have into hell if he elected to hand Germany over to the bourgeoisie."

"Better to the Soviet," Von Thal grunted.

The Captain came and spoke to Von Thal in a low voice.

"It is a mistral which arrives, Your Highness," he announced.

The Prince rose to his feet and gazed westward. There was a curious bank of clouds which seemed suddenly to have appeared from nowhere. White streaks of foam danced upon the sea below. Von Thal waved the man aside with a muttered word and turned his back upon him.

"The trouble of this affair," Fawley declared, "is that the Princess has formed an exaggerated idea of my influence. I am only a pawn, after all. Berati has already a sheaf of reports from Germany. Mine will only be one of the many."

"At the risk of flattering your self-esteem," Elida said, "I will tell you that Berati has an extraordinary opinion of your resource and capacity. He does not believe that any other man breathing would have obtained for him the plan of the new French defences on the frontier, with particulars of their guns, and preserved his life and liberty."

Fawley laid down his cigarette. For once Elida had scored. He was genuinely disturbed.

"That sounds rather like a fairy-tale, Princess."

"Never mind," she persisted. "It was bad diplomacy on my part, I admit, to tell you that, but I could not resist the temptation. You are a clever man, Major Fawley, but neither I nor my friends walk altogether in the dark. You need not be afraid. Only I and two others know what I have just told you, and how you communicated with Berati is still a secret to us."

"Such an enterprise as you have alluded to," Fawley observed, "would have been more in my line. I am no politician. That is what neither my chief nor you seem to understand. I will promise what you ask," he went on, after a moment's pause. "I shall not travel to Germany with Krust. I will not be subject to his influence, and I will visit any organisations or meet anyone you may suggest."

Von Thal sprang to his feet. There was a sullen look in his face, angry words trembling upon his lips. Elida rose swiftly and laid her fingers upon his mouth.

"I forbid you to speak, Maurice," she enjoined. "You hear that? You see, I have guessed your thoughts. You would wish to provoke a quarrel with Major Fawley by means of an insult. I will not tolerate it. I accept Major Fawley's proposition. Remember, I am your superior in this matter. You must do as I say."

She withdrew her hand slowly. The blood seemed to have rushed to Von Thal's head. He was by no means a pleasant sight.

"And if I refuse?" he demanded.

"You will be ordered to return to Germany to-night," she told him. "You will never again be associated with any enterprise in which I am concerned, and I shall do my best to discredit you entirely with Von Salzenburg."

Von Thal hesitated for a moment, then he swung on his heel and strode away forward. From their sheltered seats they could see him leaning over the side of the boat regardless of the spray through which they were driving.

"A nice joy-trip you are giving me," Fawley grumbled. "How do you know that I am not liable to sea-sickness?"

"You do not seem to me to be that sort of person," she answered absently.

They were rolling and pitching now in the trough of a heavy sea. Occasionally a wave sent a cloud of spray over their heads. They had turned for the harbour, but it was hard to see more than its blurred outline. A sailor had brought them oilskins and removed the plates and glasses.

"We are running in with the wind now," Fawley remarked. "Good thing we turned when we did."

She drew him farther into the shelter. It seemed to him that her fingers lingered almost caressingly upon his wrist.

"If only you and I," she sighed, "could be on the same side."

"Well, I think I should be an improvement upon your present fellow-conspirators," he rejoined.

"Maurice, as I dare say you know," she told him, "is a nephew of Von Salzenburg. He has the reputation of being a fine soldier."

"These fine soldiers," Fawley grunted, "are always a terrible nuisance in civil life. What the mischief is he up to now?"

Conditions had changed during the last few moments. They were only about a hundred yards from the entrance to the harbour, but they seemed to be taking an unusual course which laid them broadside to the heavy seas. Two sailors were busy lowering one of the dinghies. Elida pointed towards the wheel. The Prince had taken the captain's place, he had thrown off his oilskins and coat and was standing up with the wheel in his hand, his broad ugly mouth a little open, his eyes fixed steadily upon the narrow opening to the harbour.

"He is mad!" Elida exclaimed.

A great wave broke over them, smashing some of the woodwork of the deck lounge and sending splinters of glass in every direction. People were running, dimly visible shrouded figures, through the mist and cloud of rain to the end of the pier. There were warning shouts. The captain gripped Von Thal by the arm and shouted indistinguishable words. Maurice's right hand shot out. The man staggered back and collapsed half upon the deck, half clinging to the rails. Once again they mounted a wave which for a few seconds completely engulfed them.

"Maurice is running straight for the sea wall," Elida gasped.

"In that case," Fawley exclaimed, tearing off his coat, "I think we will make for the dinghy."

There was suddenly a terrific crash, a splintering of wood all around them, a crashing and screeching of torn timbers. They seemed to be up in the air for a moment. Von Thal, who had left the wheel, came dashing towards them. The deck seemed to be parting underneath their feet. Fawley drew the girl closer into his arms, her wet cheeks were pressed to his. For a period of seconds their lips met fiercely, hungrily, the flavour of salt in their madness and the roar and blinding fury of the breaking waves stupefying them.... Once again the yacht, which had been sucked backwards, crashed into the stone wall. This time she fell apart like a cardboard box. Fawley saw as though in a dream Elida hauled into the dinghy. She was surrounded by ugly pieces of wreckage threatening them every second with death. He drew a long breath and dived down to the calmer waters.

CHAPTER XIII

FAWLEY, after several weeks of devious and strenuous wanderings, crossed the very fine hall of Berlin's most famous hotel well aware that he was now approaching the crucial point of his enterprise. Frankfurt, thanks to his English and French connections, had been easy. At Cologne and some of the smaller towns around, even if he had aroused a little suspicion, he had learnt all that he needed to know. But in Berlin, for the first time, outside aid was denied to him, and he became conscious that he was up against a powerful and well-conducted system of espionage. The very politeness of the hotel officials, their casual glance at his credentials, their meticulous care as to his comfort—all these things had seemed to him to possess a sinister undernote. He chose for his headquarters a small suite upon the sixth floor with the sitting-room between his bedroom and bathroom, but his first discovery was that the one set of keys attached to the double doors was missing, and he only obtained the keys giving access to the corridor after some considerable delay....

Yet to all appearance he had been received as an ordinary and welcome visitor. According to his custom, he was travelling under his own passport and without any sort of compromising papers, yet all the time he fancied that these polite officials, some of whom seemed to be always in the background, were looking at him from behind that masked expression of courtesy and affability with definite suspicion.

For two days he lounged about the city as an ordinary tourist without any particular attempt at secrecy, asking no questions, seeking no new acquaintances, and visiting only the largest and best-known restaurants. On the third morning after his arrival there was a thunderous knocking at the door and, in reply to his invitation to enter, there rolled in, with his fat, creaseless face and pudgy hand already extended, Adolf Krust. Fawley laid down his pipe and suffered his fingers to be gripped.

"So you gave us all the slip, you crafty fellow," the visitor exclaimed. "And you left my little friend in such distress, with a copy of an A.B.C. in her hand and tears in her eyes, and all that we know, or rather that we do not know, is that the *Daily Mail* tells us that Major Fawley, late of the American Army, has left the Hôtel de France for London. London indeed! The one place in the world that for you and me and for those like us is dead. What should you be doing in London, eh?"

"I may go there before I finish up," Fawley replied, smiling. "After all, I am half English, you know."

"You are of no country," Adolf Krust declared, sinking into the indicated easy-chair and blowing out his cheeks. "You are the monarch of cosmopolitans. You are a person who carries with him always a cult. You have upset us all in Monte Carlo. Some believe that you were drowned when that clumsy fool, that idiot nephew of Von Salzenburg's, drove you on to the sea wall of the harbour in that fearful mistral."

"It was an excellent stage disappearance for me," Fawley observed. "I was just a shade too much in the limelight for my safety or my comfort."

"You speak the truth," his visitor agreed. "Only two days after you left, the French military police were swarming in the hotel. Everyone was talking about you. There were some who insisted upon it that you were a dangerous fellow. They are right, too, every time, but all the same you breathe life. Yes," Krust concluded with a little sigh of satisfaction, "it is well put, that—you breathe life."

"Perhaps that is because I have so often loitered in the shadow of death," Fawley remarked.

Krust shrugged his tightly encased shoulders. In the city he had abandoned the informal costume of the Riviera and was attired with the grave precision of a senator.

"In the walk of life we traverse," he said, "that is a matter of course.... Ach, but this is strange!"

"What is strange?"

"To find you after all my persuadings in my beloved Berlin."

"I have also visited your beloved Frankfurt and Cologne," Fawley confided dryly, perfectly certain that his visitor was well acquainted with the fact.

The blue eyes grew rounder and rounder.

"You take away the breath," Krust declared. "As the great young man used to say—you sap the understanding. You have seen Von Salzenburg?"

Fawley shook his head.

"Not I!" he answered. "Some day, if there is anything that might come of it, we will see him together."

Krust's eyes became more protuberant than ever. This was a strange one, this man! He wondered whether, after all, Greta had told the truth, whether she had not all the time kept back something from him. Fawley pushed a box of cigarettes across the table. His caller waved them away and produced a leather receptacle the size of a traveller's sample case.

"You are not one of those who object to the odour of any good tobacco even if it be strong?" he asked. "You have seen my cigars. You will not smoke them, but they are good. They are made in Cologne and they cost two pfennig each, which in these days helps the pocket-book."

"Smoke one by all means," Fawley invited. "Thank goodness it is warm weather and the windows are open!"

"You joke at my taste in tobacco," Krust grumbled, "but you do not joke at my taste in nieces, *nicht*? What about the little Greta?"

"Charming," Fawley admitted with a smile. "Everyone in Monte Carlo wondered at your luck."

"It is all done by kindness and a little generosity," the other remarked with an air of self-satisfaction. "I have not the looks. I certainly have not the figure, but there are other gifts! One has to study the sex to know how to please."

"How did you find me out here?" Fawley asked abruptly.

"I have intelligent friends in Berlin who watch," was the cautious reply. "You were seen down south at the march of the Iron Army. You were seen at the new Russian Night Club in Düsseldorf the other night, where there are not many Russians but a good deal of conversation. People are curious just now about travellers. I have been asked what you do here."

Fawley yawned.

"Bore myself chiefly," he admitted. "I find Germany a far better governed country than I had anticipated. I have few criticisms. A great brain must be at work somewhere."

Krust rolled a cigar between his fingers. It was a light-coloured production, long, with faint yellow spots. Every few seconds he knocked away the ash.

"A great brain," he repeated, as if following out a train of thought of his own. "I will tell you something, friend Fawley. What you think is produced by a great brain is nothing but the God-given sense of discipline which every true German possesses. There is no one to thank for the smoothness with which the great wheel revolves. It is the German people themselves who are responsible."

"Prosperity seems to be returning to the country," Fawley reflected. "I find it hard to believe that these people will suffer themselves to be led into such an adventure as a new war."

Krust pinched his cigar thoughtfully.

"The German has pride," he said. "He would wish to re-establish himself. In the meantime he does not hang about at street corners. He works. You want to see underneath the crust. Why not accept my help? Unless some doors are unlocked even you, the most brilliant secret service agent of these days, will fail. You will make a false report. You will leave this country and you will not understand."

"Berati has his methods and I have mine," Fawley observed. "I admit that I am puzzled, but I do not believe that either you or Von Salzenburg could enlighten me.... Still, there would be no harm in our dining and spending the evening together. My ears are always open, even if I do not promise to be convinced."

Krust sighed.

"To go about openly with you," he regretted, "would do neither of us any good. It would give me all the joy in the world to offer you the hospitality of the city. I dare not."

Fawley smiled as he pressed the bell for the waiter.

"Then I must show you some."

Adolf Krust chuckled.

"I am a man," he confessed, "who when he talks likes to drink. Most good Germans are like that."

"Cocktails?"

Krust waved aside the idea.

"I drink cocktails only at the bar. Wine or beer here. It is equal to me."

Fawley rang the bell and gave the waiter an order. The finest Rhine wine was served to them in deliciously frosted glasses. They drank solemnly an unspoken toast. Fawley refilled the glasses. Again they were raised.

"To our better understanding," the German said.

He muttered a few words in his own language. The toast, however, whatever it may have been, was never drunk. There was a loud knocking at the outside door. What followed on Fawley's invitation to enter seemed to his astonished eyes more like the advance guard of a circus than anything. The door was thrown open with a flourish. The manager of the hotel, in a tightly fitting frock coat and grey trousers of formal design, entered hurriedly. He took not the slightest notice of Fawley, but swung round and ranged himself by the side of the threshold. He was joined a few seconds later by the assistant manager, dressed in precisely the same fashion, who also made precipitate entrance and stood on the other side facing his chief. There followed an officer dressed in some sort of uniform, and after him a younger man, who appeared to hold the post of A.D.C., in more sombre but still semi-military accoutrements. Last of all came a man in civilian clothes—stern, with a shock of brown hair streaked with grey, hard features, granite-like mouth, keen steely eyes. He held up his hand as he entered in a gesture which might have been intended for the Fascist salute or might have been an invocation to silence. He spoke German correctly, but with a strong Prussian accent.

"My name is Behrling—Heinrich Behrling," he announced. "It is my wish to speak a few words with the agent of my friend General Berati of Rome. I have the pleasure—yes?"

Fawley bowed, but shook his head.

"I cannot claim the distinction of being the recognised agent of that great man," he declared. "I am an American visiting Germany as a tourist."

The new-comer advanced further into the room and shook hands with some solemnity. Fawley turned towards where his previous visitor had been seated, then gave a little start. The hideous and unsavoury cigar propped up against an ash-tray was still alight. The arm-chair, however, had been pushed back and the black Homburg hat which had rested upon the floor had gone. There was in the place where Adolf Krust had sat the most atrocious odour of foul tobacco, but nowhere in the room was there any sign of him nor any indication of his sudden departure except the wide-opened door leading into the bathroom.

"You search for something?" the visitor asked.

"Before you came, sir," Fawley confided, "I had a caller. He must have taken his leave in a hurry."

Heinrich Behrling laughed hardly.

"There are many," he declared, "who leave in a hurry when I arrive!"

CHAPTER XIV

HEINRICH BEHRLING, the man whom the most widely read paper in Berlin had called only that morning "the underground ruler of Germany," showed no hesitation in taking the vacated easy-chair, and he watched the disappearance of the still burning cigar out of the window with an air of satisfaction. In response to a wave of the hand his escort retired. He breathed a sigh of relief.

"It gives me no pleasure to be so attended," he declared, "but what would you have? The Communists have sworn that before the end of the week I shall be a dead man. I prefer to live."

"It is the natural choice," Fawley murmured with a smile.

"You are Major Fawley, the American who has entered the service of Italy?" Behrling demanded. "You speak German—yes?"

"Yes to both questions," was the prompt reply. "My name is Fawley, I have accepted a temporary post under the Italian Government and I speak German."

"What brought you to Berlin?"

"Everyone comes to Berlin nowadays."

"You came on Berati's orders, of course."

Fawley's fingers tapped lightly upon his desk and he remained for a moment silent.

"I look upon your visit as a great honour, sir," he said. "I only regret that when I became a servant I became dumb."

"I wish there were more like you on my staff," Behrling muttered with a throaty exclamation. "Can I deal with you? That is the question."

"On behalf of whom?"

"On behalf of my country. You have seen my army in the making. You have visited Cologne and Frankfurt, amongst other towns. You know what is coming to Germany as well as I can tell you. I ask whether I can deal with you on behalf of my country."

"Is this not a little premature, Herr Behrling?" Fawley asked quietly. "The elections are yet to come."

"So you have been listening to the fat man," was the scornful reply. "The man who smokes that filthy stuff and left the room like a streak of lightning at my coming! He would have you think that the dummy who has taken my place in the Reichstag can be dealt with. He is a fool. If I raised my hand in opposition—crash tomorrow would come the whole of your brilliant scheme, and where would you be then? Where would Italy be? I ask you that."

Fawley was silent. This man was not as he had expected. He was at the same time more verbose yet more impressive.

"If I choose to listen to my councillors," Behrling went on, "I will tell you what would happen. Italy would be stripped, disgraced, convicted of a great crime and—worse still—guilty of being found out. That is what will happen to any nation who dares to ignore the only party which is strong enough to rule Germany, the only party which can put into the field an army of patriots."

Fawley shook his head regretfully.

"Alas," he explained, "I am only a messenger. I have no weight in the councils of Italy."

"You can repeat my words."

"I will do so."

"When?"

"When I return to Italy."

Behrling's expression was fervent and blasphemous.

"Why do you wait till then?" he demanded. "You are here to see how the land lies. You have to make your report. Von Salzenburg's men are veterans of the war. They would carry arms in no man's cause. Soon they will be carrying them to the grave. The young spirit of Germany is with me. Italy will miss her great chance. She will pass down into the rank of second-class nations if she does not recognise this."

"Every word of what you have said I promise shall be repeated."

"But why not in your despatches?" Behrling argued, striking the table with his fist. "Why not to-night? Why not let a special messenger fly to Rome? An aeroplane is at your disposal."

"I never send despatches," Fawley confided, tapping a cigarette upon the table and lighting it.

His visitor stared at him in blank surprise.

"What do you mean? Of course you must send despatches."

"I have never sent one in my life," Fawley assured him. "I have very seldom committed a line of anything relating to my profession to paper. When a thing is important enough for me to pass it on to my chiefs, I take the knowledge of it in my brain and I go to them."

Behrling rose to his feet and walked restlessly up and down the room. His strong features were working nervously. He threw away his cigarette. It was obvious that he had been living for months under a great strain. He beat the air with his fists—a gesture which seemed to Fawley curiously familiar. Suddenly he swung round.

"The fat man—Adolf Krust—he has been here this afternoon?"

Fawley nodded.

"Yes, he has been here. He was in Monte Carlo when I was there. He went on to see Berati. It is scarcely my business to tell you so," Fawley observed, "still, I see no reason why I should keep another man's secret. He only got as far as San Remo. Berati refused to see him."

"When do you return to Rome?"

"In ten days."

"The world itself may be changed in that time," Behrling declared impatiently. "If you were to study the welfare of your adopted country I tell you this—you would return to Rome to-morrow. You would use every argument to convince Berati that Italy stands upon the threshold of a colossal mistake."

"Mistake?" Fawley repeated.

"Give me a few hours of your time," Behrling demanded with flashing eyes, "and I will show you how great a mistake. If ever a thing was dead at heart, snapped at the roots, it is the monarchical spirit of Germany. Youth alone can rebuild and inspire Germany. These men who do the goose-step through the streets of Berlin, who have adopted the mouldy, ignoble relic of the most self-intoxicated monarchical régime which ever plunged its country into ruin, they lack everything. They lack inspiration, they lack courage, more than anything they lack youth. You have seen my men march, Major Fawley. You know that their average age is under twenty-four. There is the youth and fire of the country. There is the living force. They have no soul-fatigue."

"There are rumours," Fawley ventured to remind him, "of negotiations between the monarchists and your young men. I have heard it said that if this great cataclysm should take place, there would be a coming together of every military party in Germany."

"You may have heard this," Behrling admitted with a queer smile, "but you would not be sitting where you are now if you had not the wit to know that it is a falsehood. My men will fight for their country and their principles and me, but not a shot would they fire to drag back from their happy obscurity one half an hour of the accursed Hohenzollern rule."

"Then what do you predict will be the government in this country?" Fawley asked.

"No sane man doubts that," Behrling answered. "The people have spoken. I am on my way there already. I shall be dictator within two months. In twelve months Germany will be once more a great power, the greatest power amongst the European nations."

Fawley lit another cigarette and pushed the box towards his visitor, who, however, shook his head.

"In these days," the latter confided, "I may not smoke and I may not drink. It is the Lenten fast of my life. Every nerve of my body is strained. The time for relaxation will come afterwards. Major Fawley, I invite you to attend a meeting of my council to-night."

Fawley declined respectfully.

"If I accepted your offer," he acknowledged, "I should be doing so under false pretences. I was fortunate enough to intercept a private despatch addressed to Berati's chief last time I was in Rome. From it I am convinced that, however long she may hesitate, Italy has made up her mind to support the monarchical party. The treaty is already drawn up."

Behrling's arms went out with a gesture towards the sky. One forgot the banality of the gilt and white ceiling above his head.

"What are treaties," he cried, "when the stars are falling and new worlds are being born? You and I both know why Berati's master leans towards the monarchical party. It is because he has sworn that there shall be only one dictator in Europe. That is sheer vanity. In time his patriotism will conquer and he will see the truth.... I meet you at midnight at an address which will be given you this afternoon with no explanation. You will be there?"

"If you invite me with the full knowledge of the situation," Fawley replied.

"That is understood."

CHAPTER XV

THE maître d'hôtel at the newest Berlin restaurant, which had the reputation of almost fantastic exclusiveness, was typically Teutonic. His fair hair had been shaved close to his skull, his fierce little yellow moustache was upturned in military fashion, his protuberant stomach interfered in no manner with his consequential, almost dignified bearing. He scarcely troubled to reply to Fawley's enquiry for a table.

"Every table is taken," he announced, "for to-night and every night this week."

"For the other evenings during the week," Fawley replied, "I have no interest. Please to give the matter your attention. You had better glance at this card."

The maître d'hôtel turned ponderously around. Fawley's rather lazy voice, easily recognisable as American notwith-standing his excellent accent, was in a way impressive. A great deal more so, however, was the card which he had presented. The man's manner underwent a complete change. He indulged in a swift ceremonious bow.

"Your table is reserved, *Herr Oberst*," he said. "Please to follow me."

He led the way into a small but evidently very high-class restaurant. The walls were panelled in black oak, which, so far from giving the place a sombre appearance, increased the brilliancy of the effect produced by the masses of scarlet flowers with which every table was decorated, the spotless linen, the profusion of gleaming glass and silver. He led the way to a small table in a recess—a table laid for three, one place of which was already occupied. Fawley stopped short. Elida was seated there—looking like a Greuze picture in her filmy veil and white satin gown, her chestnut brown hair and soft hazel eyes. She was obviously very nervous.

"I am afraid that there must be some mistake," Fawley said to the maître d'hôtel. "It is a man whom I am expecting to meet."

The maître d'hôtel had resumed his consequential air.

"I do not make mistakes, *Herr Oberst*," he declared. "This is the table commanded by my most honoured patron to be reserved for Herr Oberst Fawley and the Princessin Elida di Rezco di Vasena. His Excellency will join you later."

Elida smiled appealingly up at Fawley.

"You will support my presence for a short time until your host arrives?" she begged. "He is, as you know, a very busy man. He thought that we might converse for a while until he comes."

"But what do you know about him?" Fawley asked wonderingly. "Surely this is not your *galère*?"

"I will explain," she promised. "You are angry with me, but indeed nothing that happened was my fault. Please sit down."

She laid her hand upon his wrist and drew him gently towards the table. Fawley steeled himself, as well he might, against the lure of her beseeching eyes, but took the place by her side.

"Forgive me if I seemed ungracious," he murmured. "I never dreamed of seeing you here."

She drew a sigh of relief and approved his idea of a cocktail. The pedagogue of the place strutted away. They were alone.

"Dear friend," she said, and for a person who had seemed to him, at most times, so indifferent, her voice trembled with emotion. "Indeed I was not to blame. No idea of my mad cousin's scheme had ever entered my head. One result of it you see in my presence here."

"I am glad to believe it," he answered. "Do you mean, then, that your sympathies are changed?"

"It would seem so, would it not?" she answered with a sigh of relief. "It has been a great upheaval, but I believe that they are. My cousin assured me that Von Salzenburg himself said that you were to be got rid of. The idea sickened me. I no longer wish to serve a company of assassins."

The cocktails were served. Elida ordered supper and wine.

"You see," she explained, "our host eats or drinks practically nothing. I am to entertain you till he comes. You are to be impressed. How shall I begin, I wonder?"

He raised his eyebrows.

"Princess——" he began.

"You may call me Elida," she interrupted. "From you I prefer it. I shall call you Martin. In a place like this we do not wish to advertise ourselves."

"I am very happy to find you so gracious," he assured her. "I am happy, too, to know that you did not share your cousin's desire to send me to destruction."

"No one in the world," she said quietly, "has a stronger wish than I have, Martin, to keep you alive, to keep you well, to keep you near me if I could."

"Do you speak for your new chief?" he enquired.

"You must please not be bitter," she pleaded. "I speak for myself. That, I assure you, you should believe. If you wish to be serious, I will now speak to you for Heinrich Behrling. It was his wish that I should do so."

"Why should he trouble about me?" Fawley asked, toying with the stem of his wine-glass. "I am only an agent, and a mercenary at that."

"Do not fence," she begged. "Remember that I know all about you. We can both guess why you are here. Berati is at last not absolutely certain that he is dealing with the right party. Very late in the day and against his will he is finding his wisdom—as I have. Our tinsel Prince and his goose-stepping soldiers will never help Germany towards freedom. It is the passionate youth of Germany, the liberty-loving and country-loving youth in whose keeping the future rests."

"This is very interesting," Fawley remarked with a faint smile. "Considering your antecedents I find it almost incredible."

"Must one ignore the welfare of one's country because one happens to be born an aristocrat?" she demanded.

"Not if a Rienzi presents himself," he retorted. "Are you sure, however, that Behrling really is your Rienzi?"

"If I were not," she insisted, with a note of passion in her tone, "I should never have given my life and reputation and everything worth having to his cause, as I have done since the day of that catastrophe upon the yacht. Do you know, Martin, that I am one of a band—the latest recruit, perhaps, but one of the most earnest—a band of six thousand young women all born in different walks of life. We have all the same idea. We work to make Heinrich Behrling the ruler of Germany. We are not all Germans. We do not wear uniform, we do not look for any reward. Our idea is to give everything we possess, whatever it may be—money, our gifts of persuasion, our lives if necessary—to win adherents to Behrling's cause, to stop and rout the communists and the monarchist party. Another Hohenzollern mixed up with politics and the whole world would lose faith in Germany. The only way that she can escape from the yoke of France is by showing the world that she has espoused the broader and greater principles of life and government."

Fawley accepted a cigarette.

"You are very interesting, Elida," he said. "I wish that I knew more of this matter. I am afraid that I am a very dumb and ignorant person."

"It has occurred to me once or twice this evening," she rejoined dryly, "that you wish to appear so."

"Alas," he sighed, "I can assure you that I am no actor."

"Nor are you, I am afraid," she whispered, leaning across the table, "quite so impressionable as I fancied you were that afternoon in the corridor of Berati's Palazzo."

The grim lines at the corners of his mouth relaxed.

"Elida," he replied, as he looked into her eyes, "all I can say is—give me the opportunity to prove myself."

She was puzzled for a moment. Then she smiled.

"You are thinking of Krust and his little crowd of fairies," she laughed. "Yet I am told that he finds them very useful. One of them you seemed to find—rather attractive—at Monte Carlo."

He shrugged his shoulders. Perhaps she realised that her mention of the place was not altogether tactful. She changed the conversation.

"Why are you not working for your own country?" she asked curiously.

"Because my own country has a passion for imagining that even in these days of fast steamships and seaplanes she can remain apart from Europe and European influence," he answered, with a faintly regretful tremor in his tone. "We have abandoned all Secret Service methods. We have no Secret Service. I can tell you of six departments in which one might have served before the war. Not one of these exists to-day. In their place we have one so-called Intelligence Office, the only qualification to belong to which is that a man has never been out of his own country, can speak no language but his own, and is devoid of any pretensions to intelligence! The work for its own sake is so fascinating that one finds it hard to abandon it altogether. That is why I offered my services to Italy."

"And are you satisfied? The work interests you?"

He seemed a little doubtful.

"Lately," he admitted, "there is too much talk and too little action. I cannot see that I make any definite progress."

"That means that you weary yourself talking to me?" she asked, her hand resting for a moment on his and her deliriously soft eyes pleading with him.

"Not in the least," he assured her. "In a few minutes, though, we shall have our friend Behrling here and it will all begin again. I would so much sooner take you somewhere else where Behrling is not likely to appear and ask you a few questions which you would find quite easy to answer."

A brilliant smile parted her lips.

"Now you talk more as I had hoped," she confided. "Indeed, if you would let me I would wish to be your companion all the time that you are here. All the devotion I can offer is at your command, but I will be honest with you—there are still a few things I want to know."

"Elida," he said, "I do not believe that there is a single thing in the world I could tell you that you do not know already. For instance, heaps of people must have told you that you have the most beautiful hazel-brown eyes in the world."

She patted his hand.

"If I were Nina or Greta," she observed, "I should throw my arms around your neck. You would wish it—yes?"

It was a very beautiful arm, but he shook his head.

"It is absurd of me," he confessed, "but I should be afraid that you were not sincere."

"How very Anglo-Saxon!" she meditated. "What on earth has sincerity to do with it?"

"To the sentimentalist——" he began.

"My dear new friend Martin," she interrupted, "do not let us spoil everything before we begin. We are neither of us sentimentalists. We are both just playing a game: fortunately it is a pleasant game. I am afraid that you mean to win. Never mind, there are pleasures—— But do not speak about sentiment. That belongs to the world we leave behind us when we take our country into our hearts."

"The wrong word, I suppose," he admitted. "On the other hand, I do confess to being a trifle maudlin. If I had any secrets to give away, you would succeed where Behrling would fail."

"But you have none?"

"Not a ghost of one," he assured her.

Her face suddenly lost its softened charm. She was looking past him towards the door. He leaned forward and followed her gaze; then, though nothing audible escaped his lips, he whistled softly to himself. It was Krust who had entered with Fräulein Nina, Krust in bulging white shirt-front and waistcoat, his dinner-coat tightly stretched across the shoulders, his beautifully shaven face pink and white, his hair brushed smoothly back. He recognised Fawley instantly. He deposited his companion at their table and made his way up the room. For the first part of his progress the most beatifically welcoming smile parted his lips. Then he saw Elida and the good humour faded from his face. His lips took an unpleasant curve, his eyes seemed to recede into his head. Again the mask fell. He came towards them with outstretched hands. The smile re-established itself.

"My friend Fawley," he exclaimed. "I have an opportunity, then, of making my apologies for leaving your salon so abruptly. An engagement of the utmost importance came into my mind as I heard your friends at the door."

He shook hands with Fawley and looked questioningly at Elida.

"I believe, Princess," he ventured, with a stiff bow, "that I have had the pleasure."

She shook her head.

"I am afraid that you are mistaken," she said coldly.

Krust was not in the least discomposed. He pointed down the room to where Nina waved her hand gaily at Fawley.

"My work here is finished," he confided. "Others more capable are taking it over. I return to-morrow to Monte Carlo. The thought of it has made the little one very happy. And you, my friend?"

"I am never sure of my movements," was the vague reply.

"If I had not found you so charmingly occupied," Krust continued, "I would ask you to join us."

"As you see, it is impossible," Fawley pointed out, a trifle curtly.

Krust, his good humour apparently completely restored, took his leave. He had only proceeded a few steps, however, when he came to a pause on the edge of the dancing-floor. There was the sound of commotion from the entrance hall of the place, a tangle of angry voices, a peremptory command given in an official tone, a glimpse of grey uniforms and the flash of arms. The music stopped, the dancers at that end of the room hurried towards the doorway. Krust followed their example, but he was too late. A heavy black curtain which hung over the entrance was drawn by some unseen hand, the sound behind was partially deadened. Suddenly the manager pushed the curtains back and appeared upon the floor.

"Ladies and gentlemen, honourable clients of mine," he announced, "the slight disturbance outside is over. Kindly resume your seats. Some young men, members of a recently inaugurated society, endeavoured to enter in uniform—which is strictly against the rules. The police interfered and they have been sent to their homes."

There was a brief silence. Few people understood the exact nature of the disturbance. Here and there, however, was an angry snarl of voices. The veins were standing out on Krust's forehead. He strode up to the manager in a fury.

"Who sent for the police?" he demanded.

"There was no need to send for them," was the prompt reply. "The young gentlemen were followed here from the gardens."

"Did you refuse them entrance to your restaurant?" Krust persisted.

Everyone seemed to be holding their breaths. There was a queer strained silence in the luxurious little place.

"It is against the law for anyone to enter wearing an unrecognised uniform," the manager declared. "I told them so. Whilst we were discussing the matter the police appeared."

"You will bow down to that uniform before many days have passed," Krust prophesied furiously.

"Ach, that or another!" was the equally angry reply.

Krust stepped forward as though to deal a blow. Nina, who had left her place, silently threw her arms around his neck. She whispered something in his ear. He suffered himself to be led away. The orchestra struck up again. The dancing recommenced....

"Behold," Elida exclaimed, as she watched the waiter filling her glass with champagne, "a tableau! A situation which might have become more than dramatic. Krust—the monarchist spy—with one of his little butterflies. Major Fawley, the Italian mercenary, the trusted agent of Berati. I, Elida di Rezco di Vasena, who have gone over at the peril of my life to the new order. We line the walls of this restaurant. What are we playing at? I scarcely know. We are all just a little hysterical these days. The restaurant is likely to be raided by the Communists if Behrling comes, by the monarchists if the refusal to admit those officers is reported at their headquarters, or by Behrling's own men. What will our friend Berati say when he hears that you have been seen in such an environment?"

"He will probably realise," Fawley replied, "that I am going about my business and his in my own way. Mercenaries, as I dare say you know, are never over-officered. They are left with a certain measure of initiative. If one were to indulge in speculations," he went on, after a momentary pause, "one might wonder what Krust does here. From the fact that Behrling suggested it as a rendezvous one might gather that this place is frequented by his followers. Is it not a little dangerous in these days when party spirit is running high to risk an encounter?"

Elida shrugged her pearly white shoulders.

"Krust can take care of himself," she said. "He is, as I dare say you have heard, the richest man in Germany, and he is reputed to have a secret body of armed guards, some of whom are never far distant. In any case the present situation has all developed in a week. This was Von Salzenburg's headquarters before Behrling decided to establish himself here. A month ago Gustaf there was bowing to other lords."

For the second time that evening some measure of commotion was manifest at the entrance. This time, however, there was no intimation of any dispute. A great man was being welcomed. Heinrich Behrling, in plain evening clothes, handed his overcoat and soft black hat to an attendant and followed Gustaf's outstretched hand towards the table where Fawley and his companion were seated.

CHAPTER XVI

FAWLEY watched his approaching host with calm and critical interest. His travels in the country during the last few days had already convinced him that great events were looming. A tortured nation was on the point of breaking its bonds. An atmosphere of impending cataclysm was brooding over the place. The worn faces of the people, the continuous stream of processions, the crowded cafés, all gave evidence of it. It was as though there were dynamite upon the pavements and liquid dynamite in the air, dynamite which needed only a spark to light the storm. Even in this luxurious and secluded restaurant Fawley thought that the first mutterings of the thunder might begin.... Looking across the room he saw the good-natured expression fade from the face of Adolf Krust, the great industrialist, and saw his eyes receding into his head, alight as they were with hatred, saw the menacing curve of his lips as he stared at the approaching figure. Elida touched her companion on the arm.

"You see what is happening," she whispered. "Every other table in the restaurant has an engaged card upon it. Now watch."

Without any confusion or haste a well-behaved, good-looking crowd of young men, with here and there a woman companion, had followed Behrling into the place. Every one knew his table and occupied it swiftly. They wore no sort of uniform, these new-comers. They were dressed with singular precision in the fashion of the day, but there was a small brown ribbon upon the lapel of their dinner-coats. Furthermore, although they were of varying types, there was a curious similitude in their bearing and expression.

"Interesting," Fawley murmured. "I gather that these young men have all been subjected to some sort of military training?"

"They are Behrling's bodyguard," she confided. "It is not his own idea, it is the idea of those who would protect him. Krust to-night, for instance, might easily have made mischief. What chance has he now? He has not been allowed a table within fifty feet of us, and his slightest movement will be watched."

She rose to her feet to welcome the new-comer. Fawley followed her example. Behrling, still without a smile upon his strong, colourless face, bowed formally to them both and sank into the vacant chair.

"You have been entertained, I hope, Major Fawley?" he asked.

"Admirably," the other assured him.

"You will remember that you are my guests," he went on. "Supper, I think, has been already ordered. You will forgive me if I drink nothing but coffee and eat some plain food.

I see," he added, glancing across the room, "that our friends the enemy are represented here to-night."

Elida nodded.

"Adolf Krust has been over to speak to us," she remarked. "He looks upon Major Fawley as a lamb in danger of straying from the fold."

"I hear that he was at the Italian Embassy this evening," Behrling confided. "Does that disconcert you, Major Fawley?"

"Not in the least," was the composed reply. "The work of investigation which I have to do I shall do in my own way and in my own fashion. Krust will not interfere with or influence me."

"You are in a difficult position," Behrling continued, as he watched the glasses being refilled with champagne and sipped his own coffee. "Italy is employing you upon a very delicate mission because a great scheme has been thought out to the last details and an unexpected crisis has imperilled its fruition. There have arisen the questions—Who is Germany? What is Germany? Who shall speak for her? Who is there alive to-day who can sign a treaty in her name?"

"These are all matters for statesmen," Fawley observed. "Very difficult matters for an outsider to deal with."

Behrling's tightened lips concealed his irritation. This impenetrable American was getting upon his nerves.

"You are here, I presume, to report upon the situation," he said. "All that I desire is that you will report upon it fairly. You saw, perhaps, the goose-step march of the weary veterans on their celebration day. What you saw was a true and just allegory. The weariness of those who fainted by the wayside—and there were many—is typical of the weariness of all the things they represent. How much you have seen of my people I do not know, but I make you this offer. I will make over to you one of my most trusted lieutenants and, with the Princess here as your guide, you shall visit the chosen spots of my country. You shall judge for yourself of the new spirit. You will be in a position then to tell those who employ you with whom it would be politic to deal."

"If you only see half as much as I have seen within the last few weeks," Elida intervened, "it will be enough."

"You must please understand this," Fawley said firmly, "I honestly do not believe that any word I could say would influence Berati or those who stand behind him in the least. He trusts none of his army of spies. He listens to every scrap of information we bring him and he decides for himself."

"Yes, but the great thing is to see that the spirit of the country is represented to him fairly," Behrling declared passionately. "Can you not see that? Krust, they tell me, although he is not in favour just now, has been twice received in Rome—once at the Vatican. I know that for a fact."

"Krust must be received wherever he claims the entrée," Fawley pointed out. "I suppose he still remains the greatest industrialist in Central Europe."

"He is also unfortunately the intimate friend of Von Salzenburg and his Royal patron," was Behrling's grim comment. "I am not pleading for myself. I am pleading only for the thousands of Germans who must go once more to their doom if a false note is struck now. They think in Rome that Germany is leaning towards the idea of a monarchy. She is doing nothing of the sort. When these clouds are cleared away, and believe me it will not be long, her programme will be before the world for everyone to see. Heart and soul she is nationalist. She is for a re-established and almighty Germany. She is for the peace that brains and industry can ensure."

A note was handed to Behrling. He read it and glanced meaningly at Elida.

"I think that our host would like to speak with some of his friends," she said. "Will you dance for a few minutes, Major Fawley?"

Fawley looked enquiringly at his host. The latter's acquiescence was swift.

"I see there two of my party with whom I have affairs," he said. "Do not leave me without a farewell, Major, or without giving me your decision. Remember, I shall expect nothing but a favourable one."

Fawley felt his feet upon the earth again. Elida, notwithstanding the smooth grace of her movements, clung to him every now and then as though he represented destiny, as though he were the only pillar of security remaining in a world threatening flood. Fawley, whose complete humanity was one of the possible elements of his success in his profession, felt her allure without the slightest idea of yielding to it.

"You must accept Heinrich Behrling's offer," she whispered eagerly. "You would not be doing your duty to the country which employs you if you did not. We can go to all the important places the very names of which are seldom mentioned in the papers nowadays. We can go by aeroplane. One of Behrling's warmest supporters is the largest maker of aeroplanes in Europe."

"What do you expect to gain from me at the end of it?" he asked, genuinely a little puzzled.

"Cannot you see," she murmured passionately, "that this German-Italian scheme would mean the reconstruction of Europe? It would bring power and supremacy to both nations and would place them where they have a right to belong. Behrling is terribly afraid that Berati's leanings are towards the other party and that he will not conclude a treaty with anyone else."

"I can understand that part of it," Fawley assented, "but I am certain that my own importance in the matter is overrated. I am here on a special errand concerning which I have to make a detailed report. Berati does not ask me for my views upon the situation. The Italian Government are satisfied with their own correspondents here. I should simply be butting in if I went home with a lot of information which they have probably already acquired."

"But they have not," she insisted, with a fierce little clutch at his arm. "There was never a man in this world—a clever man, I mean—so befooled by another as Berati's master has been by Krust. If Berati only knew the truth, there would be no further hesitation. Now listen. I must tell you more about Heinrich Behrling. I must tell you more about the monarchists here. Do you suppose that I, who am connected with three of the Royal families of Europe, who have nothing but monarchists' blood in my veins, could turn aside if I were not utterly and completely convinced? Come this way."

She led him into a little recess, pushed back the curtain and showed the way into a small but wonderfully decorated and luxurious bar. A fat and genial-looking dispenser of drinks stood behind the counter. Elida ordered champagne frappé and drew Fawley down on to a divan. He indulged in a dubious grimace.

"I was rather enjoying that dance with you," he complained.

"Have not I offered you," she reminded him, in a voice which shook with earnestness, "all the dancing with me you might care for all the days of your life? I am sincere, too.

I want many things from you, but first of all I want you to take that journey with me."

"If I took it," he told her, "if you convinced me, as you very likely might, if I flew straight back to Rome and showed Berati the whole truth, I am not sure that it would make one particle of difference. You probably know the man—he takes advice from no one and he is very seldom wrong."

"Take me to him, then," she begged. "I am forbidden the country, but I will risk that. I tried to take his life, but I will risk his retaliation."

Fawley tried to impart a lighter note to a conversation which was becoming too highly charged with emotion.

"I would not dream of doing such a thing," he said. "I have heard something of Berati's methods with Italian ladies!"

She sipped her wine with a little gesture of despair. Fawley's feet beat time to the music. She ignored the hint. Suddenly, as though by an impatient hand, the curtain shielding the other entrance to the bar was drawn back. A tall, middle-aged man of dissipated appearance, but still slim and alert in his manner, hastened across the room towards Elida, bowed in perfunctory fashion and broke into a stream of rapid German. Two or three younger men also pushed their way into the bar and ranged themselves by his side. Elida rose slowly to her feet, curtsied and resumed her place.

"You are a disgrace to your name and your family," the angry new-comer wound up. "Of your relationship I am ashamed."

"The shame is on my side," Elida answered indignantly. "I should feel it, in any case, of even an acquaintance who would attempt to brawl with a woman in a public place. If you have anything to say to me which you have not already said through Von Salzenburg and Maurice von Thal, please find another opportunity."

"What are you doing with this American?" the other demanded.

"That is entirely my affair."

"I am inclined to make it mine," was the sullen reply. "Americans are not welcome in Germany just now. We wish to be left alone to settle our own affairs."

"You do not like Americans?" Fawley asked softly.

"I *hate* them."

"Perhaps that is to be understood," Fawley observed. "Unfortunately I am in the same position with regard to Germans—of your type. I don't exactly see what we can do about it."

There was a tense silence for a moment. Outside in the restaurant the music, too, had paused. It was as though everyone had recognised the fact that there was trouble afoot. One of the younger men in the group stepped forward and tendered his card to Fawley. The latter made no movement towards taking it.

"Sir," the intervener declared, "you have insulted one who does me the honour to regard me as a friend. You insult me also if you refuse my card."

"What am I to do with your card?" Fawley asked.

"You give me yours," the other replied with a flash in his eyes. "By to-morrow morning you will know."

Fawley accepted the card, tore it in two and flung the pieces from him.

"It is time the world had finished with such theatrical trash," he observed calmly. "I happen to have earned the right to refuse to fight with anyone, as you can see for yourself if you consult an American Army List. In the meantime I suggest that you allow me to take the Princess to her table and I will return to discuss the matter with you."

Elida passed her hand through his arm. She knew most of these men who had entered and she was very determined that Fawley should leave with her.

"Since you have reminded me of our relationship," she said, turning towards the man who had first addressed her, "let me beg you, for the sake of your name, to avoid anything like a brawl. Major Fawley is a distinguished guest and I believe a well-wisher of your country."

The music outside was still silent, but there was a curious shuffling of feet upon the dancing floor. The main curtain was abruptly thrown back, a party of the young men who had followed Behrling into the restaurant made their appearance. They entered quietly without any sign or word of menace, but they were a formidable-looking body as they ranged themselves around the bar. By some manœuvre, or it may have been by chance, they spread themselves out between Elida and her angry relative. In dead silence, although to the accompaniment of a cloud of evil looks, Fawley and his companion passed out of the room.

CHAPTER XVII

ALMOST before they had stepped on to the dancing-floor the shock came. There was the sound of a shrill, penetrating whistle from a distant corner, two sharp revolver shots, and within another second the whole room was enveloped in darkness. For a moment or two the music continued, the dancers swayed into one another, a moving phalanx of half-laughing, half-terrified humanity, groping their way through the perfumed obscurity. Then a woman's hysterical cry following those two reports struck a note of fear. Somewhere in the middle of the floor a woman had fainted, calling out wildly as she collapsed.... A powerful hand gripped Fawley's arm, a man's voice whispered in his ear:

"I lead you. Hold my wrist and the Princess."

Fawley for a moment hesitated. It was obvious that there was some sort of trouble on hand. Elida whispered in his ear.

"It is Gustaf who speaks. Do anything he says."

Behind them in the darkness was the sound of something which was like a concerted movement—the steady shuffling of purposeful feet. From the corner near where they had been seated and in the vicinity of which the two shots had been fired they could hear the low moaning of a wounded man. Someone on the dancing-floor lit a briquet and thrust the tiny flame almost into the faces of the man and woman by his side, only to blow it out quickly as though he realised that the two were not the people whom he sought. Fawley hesitated no longer. With his arm still around Elida he suffered himself to be led between the tables towards the side exit and down a passage leading into the street. Underneath the flare of an electric standard a line of cars was ranged along the kerb. Gustaf opened the door of one and literally pushed them inside. The car moved off at once. A familiar voice greeted them from the corner.

"My dear Princess and Major Fawley, I owe you the most profound apologies. Gustaf is in despair. His restaurant has practically been seized by the members of a political party who would be delighted to involve me in a scandal—or worse."

"We heard shots," Fawley remarked.

"They were meant for me," Behrling said grimly. "Gustaf had a secret message and he hurried me off. It is not for myself I fear. It is for the cause."

"Who was responsible for putting out the light?" Elida asked.

"An asinine crowd of young bloods," Behrling replied contemptuously, "all blindly following that middle-aged roué. As a matter of fact, it was the best thing that could happen for us. Gustaf was able the easier to manœuvre our departure. By the by, Fawley, if this is going to be the bad night that they threatened us with, what about putting you down at your Embassy?"

Fawley shook his head.

"Sorry," he regretted. "For the moment I am not engaged in my country's interests. I can claim no privileges."

"You are not by any chance in disgrace with your own people?" Behrling asked curiously.

"Not in the least," Fawley assured him. "I simply asked for a job, found there was nothing doing and took on a mission of observation for a friendly Power."

Behrling nodded.

"What happened in the bar?" he asked abruptly.

"Nothing really happened," Fawley replied with a smile. "Nothing except threats, that is to say. A gentleman of the student type offered me his card and reminded me of the ancient institution of duelling."

"What did you do with it?"

"He tore it up," Elida intervened.

Behrling nodded approval.

"In the new Germany," he muttered, "there will be no duels. The blood of every citizen will be needed for the nation."

"You think that there will be war?" Fawley asked.

Behrling peered curiously through the obscurity of the vehicle.

"Is that not already determined upon? There may be war, and, unless Berati makes the one unpardonable mistake, the map of Europe will be altered. I have no more to say. Here is your destination. You have made me no promises, Major Fawley. You have spoken no word of approval. You have given me no hint as to where your sympathies lie. Yet I have a feeling of satisfaction. I am glad that we have met."

He shook hands warmly. Fawley turned to make his adieux to Elida. She too, however, was preparing to descend.

"I am staying with my aunt, who has a suite here," she explained.

Behrling leaned forward from his corner.

"Before we meet again, Major Fawley," he prophesied, "there will be a great change in this city—in this country. You are here now in these terrifying moments before the storm, when the air is sulphurous and over-charged with the thunders to come. You will find us a saner country when you return."

There was the sound of music and many voices as they arrived on the fourth floor. At the end of the corridor was a vision of bowing servants, and beyond, rooms banked with flowers and waving palms. Elida gave one look and stepped swiftly back into the lift.

"I cannot bear it," she told Fawley. "My aunt receives her political friends on Thursday evenings and to-night they are all there in force. I can hear their voices even here. They will tear themselves to pieces before they have finished. There must be, it seems, a hundred different ways of saving Germany and every one of my aunt's friends has hold of a different plan. Let me come and sit with you for a few minutes. I heard the waiter say that he had placed a note in your salon, so I feel that I may come without compromising you."

"By all means," Fawley assented. "My sitting-room is not much, but from the window one has at least a fine view of the city. Come with the greatest pleasure, but," he went on, as they stepped out of the lift and he fitted the key in the door of his suite, "do let us leave politics alone for a time. My sympathies are of no use to anyone. I cannot turn them into action."

She sighed as she followed him into the rooms and allowed her cloak to slip from her shoulders.

"It is too bad," she lamented, "because there was never a time in her history when Germany more needed the understanding of intelligent Anglo-Saxons. So this is where you live?"

He smiled.

"For a few hours longer," he reminded her. "I am off to-morrow."

"To Rome?"

He remained silent for a moment.

"In these days of long-distance telephones and wireless a poor Government messenger never knows where he will be sent."

He picked up the despatch which lay upon the table and, after a questioning glance towards her, opened it. He read it carefully, then tore it into small pieces.

"Your plans are changed?" she asked.

"Only confirmed," he answered. "Come and sit before the window and look down at this beautiful city. We have an idea in America, you know, or rather we used to have when I was interested in politics, that in order to bring about a state of bankruptcy in Berlin the people beautified their city, built new boulevards, new public buildings, and then failed to pay the interest on their loans!"

"It is probably true," Elida assented. "That was all before I took any interest in this part of the world. To-day Germany is on her feet again, her hands are uplifted, she is feeling for the air. She is trying to drag down from the heavens the things that belong to her. Germany has a great future, you know, Major Fawley."

"No one doubts that," he replied.

She looked around the room curiously and last of all at him, at his drawn but wholesome-looking face, his deep-set visionary eyes, his air of immense self-control. She took note of all the other things which appeal to a woman, the little wave in his hair brushed back by the ears, the humorous lines about his firm mouth. He possessed to the fullest extent the distinction of the class to which they both belonged.

"Do you mind if I become very personal for a few moments?" she asked abruptly.

"So long as you do not find too much fault with me."

"The men in the Secret Service whom I have come across," she began, "our Italian Secret Service I mean, of course, and the French, travel under false names, generally assuming a different status to their real one. They travel with little luggage, they stay in weird hotels in streets that no one ever heard of, and life for them seems to be filled with a desire to escape from their own personality. Here are you staying in the best-known hotel in Berlin under your own name, wearing the clothes and using the speech of your order. There on your writing-table is your dressing-case fitted with an ordinary lock and with your name in full stamped upon it. I begin to think that you must be a fraud. I should not be surprised to find that your proper name even was inscribed in the hotel register."

"Guilty to everything," he confessed, pushing his chair a little nearer to hers and closer to the window. "But then you must remember that the Secret Service of the old order has gone out. The memoirs writer and the novelist have given away our fireworks. We are only subtle now by being terribly and painfully obvious."

"You may be speaking the truth," she murmured, "but it seems to me that it must be a dangerous experiment. I could recall to myself the names of at least a dozen people who know that a Major Fawley is here on behalf of a certain branch of the Italian Government to see for himself and report upon the situation. It would be worth the while of more than one of them to make sure that you never returned to Rome."

"There are certain risks to be run, of course," he admitted. "The only point is that I came to the conclusion some years ago that one runs them in a more dignified fashion and with just as much chance of success by abandoning the old methods."

She sat perfectly silent for some time. They were both looking downwards at the thronged and brilliantly lit streets, the surging masses of human beings, listening to the hoarse mutterings of voices, punctuated sometimes with the shouting of excited pedestrians. There was a certain tenseness underneath it all. The trampling of feet upon the pavement was like the breaking of an incoming tide. One had the idea of mighty forces straining at a yielding leash. Elida swung suddenly round.

"You play the game of frankness wonderfully," she said bitterly, "but there are times when you fall down."

"As for instance?"

"When you make enquiries of the concierge about the air services to Rome. When you send for a Time Table to compare the trains, and when you slip into the side entrance at Cook's in the twilight an hour or so later and take your ticket for England!"

"You have had me followed?" he asked.

"It has been necessary," she told him. "What has England to do with your report to Berati?"

His eyes seemed to be watching the black mass of people below, but he smiled reflectively.

"What an advertisement this last *coup* of yours is for the open methods of diplomacy!" he observed. "Would it surprise you very much to know that I can take the night plane to Croydon, catch the International Airways to Rome and be there a little quicker than any way I have discovered yet of sailing over the Alps?"

"Will you turn your head and look at me, please?"

He obeyed at once.

"You are not going to London then?" she persisted. "Berati has abandoned that old idea of his of seeking English sympathies?"

Fawley rose to his feet and Elida's heart sank. She knew very well that during the last few minutes, ever since, in fact, she had confessed to her surveillance over him, she had lost everything she had striven so hard to gain. Her bid for his supreme confidence had failed. Before she actually realised what had happened she was moving towards the door. He was speaking meaningless words, his tone, his expression had changed. All the humanity seemed to have left his face. Even the admiration which had gleamed more than once in his eyes, and the memory of which she had treasured all the evening, had become the admiration of a man for an attractive doll.

"You are under your own roof," he remarked, as he opened the door. "You will forgive me if I do not offer to conduct you to your aunt's apartment?"

He bent over her cold fingers.

"Why are you angry with me?" she asked passionately.

He looked at her with a gleam of sadness in his eyes, the knob of the door in his hand.

"My dear Elida," he expostulated, "you know very well that the only feeling I dare permit myself to have for you is one of sincere admiration."

CHAPTER XVIII

HIS EXCELLENCY the Marchese Marius di Vasena, Ambassador from Italy to the Court of St. James's, threw himself back in his chair and held out his hands to his unexpected visitor with a gesture of astonishment. He waved his secretary away. It had really been a very anxious week and this was a form of relaxation which appealed to him.

"Elida!" he exclaimed, embracing his favourite niece. "What on earth does this mean? I saw pictures of you last week with all the Royalties at Monte Carlo. Has your aunt any idea?"

"Not the slightest," Elida laughed.

"But how did you arrive?"

"Oh, I just came," she replied. "I did not arrive direct. I had some places to visit on the way. As a matter of fact, I left Monte Carlo a fortnight ago. Yesterday I was in Paris, but I had a sudden feeling that I must see you, dear Uncle. So here I am!"

"And the need for all this haste?" the Ambassador asked courteously, as he arranged an easy-chair for his niece. "If one could only believe that it was impatience to see your elderly but affectionate relative!"

She laughed—a soft, rippling effort of mirth.

"I am always happy to see you, my dear Uncle, that you know," she assured him. "That is why I was so unhappy when you were given London. Yesterday, however, a great desire swept over me."

"And that was?"

"To attend the American Ambassador's dance to-night at Dorrington House. I simply could not resist it. Aunt will not mind. You are going to be very good-natured and take me—yes?"

The smile faded from the Ambassador's face.

"I suppose that can easily be arranged," he admitted. "It will not be a very gay affair, though. In diplomatic circles it is rather our close season."

Elida—she was certainly a very privileged niece—leaned forward and drew out one of the drawers of her uncle's handsome writing-table. She helped herself to a box of cigarettes and lit one.

"Yet they tell me," she confided, "I heard it even in Monte Carlo, that just now England or Washington—no one is certain which—perhaps both, is busy forging thunderbolts."

"No news of it has come my way," the Ambassador declared with a benevolent smile. "If one were ever inclined to give credence to absurd rumours one would rather look nearer home for trouble."

She leaned over and patted his cheek.

"Dear doyen of all the diplomats, it is not you who would tell your secrets to a little chatterbox of a niece! It seems a pity; for I love being interested."

"*Carissima*," he murmured, "to-night at Dorrington House you will find ten or a dozen terribly impressionable young Americans, two or three of them quite fresh from Washington. You will find English statesmen even who have the reputation of being sensitive to feminine charms such as yours and who have not the accursed handicap of being your uncle. You will find my own youthful staff of budding diplomats who all imagine that they have secrets locked away in their bosoms far more wonderful than any which have been confided to me. You will be in your glory, dear Elida, and if you find out anything really worth knowing about these thunderbolts, do not forget your poor relations!"

She made a little grimace at him.

"You have always been inclined to make fun of me, have you not, since I became a serious woman?"

The Marchese assumed an austere air and tone.

"I do not make fun of you," he assured her. "If I am not too happy to see you wrapped up in things which should be left to your elders, it is because there is no excitement without danger, and it was not intended that a young woman so highly placed, so beautiful as you, should court danger."

"Me—court danger?" she exclaimed with wide-open eyes.

The Ambassador's gesture dismissed her protest with a shade of impatience.

"You have the misfortune, my dear niece," he continued, "to be by birth and education an amazing example of modern cosmopolitanism. Your sister is married to a German Princeling whose father is aiming at being Chancellor of Germany and who is himself a prominent figure in this latest upheaval. Your aunt is almost the only remaining French aristocrat who is permitted to interest herself—behind the scenes, naturally—in French politics. Both your brothers, my nephews, have made their mark in our own country and are reported to be ambitious."

"Is all this the prelude to a eulogy or a lecture?" Elida asked.

"Neither," her uncle answered. "It is just that I am going to take the privilege of a near relative and an elderly man, who has at any rate won his spurs in diplomacy, to give you a word of advice. There is no place to-day, no seemly and dignified place, for women in the underground galleries of diplomacy. Spies there must always be and always have been. Cocottes have generally been the most successful, but I need not remind you of their inevitable fate. The profession is not elastic enough to include members of the great families of Europe."

There was a brief silence. A puff of wind stole into the room through the open windows, bent the lilac blossoms in their vases and wafted their perfume into the further recesses of the stately apartment. A Louis XVI clock of blue and gold inlay chimed the hour merrily. Elida moved uneasily in her chair. No one in the world had ever spoken to her like this.

"What have you been hearing about me?" she asked.

The Marchese shrugged his shoulders.

"One hears," he murmured. "One does not necessarily listen. Now, if you take my advice you will present yourself to your aunt. She is resting for a time in her rooms and taking a new face treatment from some New York wizard. She will like to know that you are here. By the by, we dine at home—only one or two very dull people—and we leave for Dorrington House at ten-thirty."

She gave his arm a gentle squeeze and kissed his forehead.

"I have sent my maid to see which are my rooms," she said. "As soon as I have had a bath I will present myself. Perhaps Aunt Thérèse will hand over the new treatment to me. A dignified and unadorned middle-age is all the mode nowadays."

"You go and tell her so," her uncle remarked with a smile.

The Marchese suffered from a fit of unusual restlessness after the departure of his favourite niece. He left his chair and paced the room, his hands behind his back, an anxious frown upon his forehead. He was an exceedingly handsome man of the best Italian type, but he seemed during the last few months to have grown older. The lines in his face were deeper, his forehead was furrowed, he had even acquired a slight stoop. He was a conscientious politician and withal an astute one. There were certain features of the present situation which filled him with uneasiness. He took up the house telephone and spoke rapidly in Italian. In a few minutes a quietly dressed young man presented himself. He carried a locked volume under his arm. The Ambassador summoned the servant who brought him in.

"Close all the windows," he ordered. "See that I am not disturbed until I ring the bell."

The man obeyed with the swiftness of the well-trained Italian. The Ambassador reseated himself at his desk. He took a key from his chain and unlocked the volume.

"The Princess Elida has arrived, Ottavio," he confided.

The young man assented.

"So I understood, Your Excellency."

The Ambassador turned over the pages of the volume which he had opened and paused at a closely written sheet.

"A fortnight ago," he continued quietly, "my niece was in Berlin. I see your reports are all unanimous. She appears to have deserted Von Salzenburg and to have left the Prince behind her in Monaco."

"That is true, Your Excellency."

"She spent much of her time with Behrling and with an American who is reported to be in the service of Berati."

"I can vouch for the truth of that, Your Excellency."

"The American arrived unexpectedly in London a few days ago," the Ambassador went on. "You brought me word of his coming, although he has not presented himself here. Perhaps that is policy. Do you know what he has been doing in the capital?"

"It is possible to ascertain, Your Excellency. His movements did not come within the scope of my observations."

The Ambassador nodded. He read through another page, then he carefully locked up the volume and returned it.

"It would appear," he remarked, "that my niece's sympathies, at any rate, have been transferred to Behrling. One might consider her almost an opportunist."

"Behrling to-day," the young man said firmly, "is the master of Germany."

The Ambassador handed him back the volume and sighed.

"That will do, Ottavio," he said. "I should like, during the next few days, to have an interview arranged with the American Ambassador."

"The matter shall be attended to, Excellency. In the meantime, I am charged with a somewhat serious communication from the Captain Vardini, Commander Borzacchi and Air Pilot Gardone. They desire to know whether they may pay their respects or whether it would be better for them to take leave of absence without announcement."

Again there was silence. The Marchese looked up wearily. He seemed suddenly conscious of the gloom of the apartment with its drawn curtains and closed windows.

"It was a message by wireless a few hours ago, Excellency. They would wish, subject to your permission, to attend the ball at Dorrington House to-night and to leave separately before morning."

"I have no jurisdiction," the Marchese pronounced. "They must obey such orders as they have received. Have you any further information?"

"None, Your Excellency, except a hint that the urgency is not so great as might seem. About the middle of next week, perhaps, we may expect official news. Is it permitted to ask Your Excellency a question?"

"With the proviso that he answers it only if he feels inclined to," was the weary reply.

"The Department has received a very cautiously worded enquiry as to this American, Major Martin Fawley," the young man confided. "It seems that he has been in Rome and on the French Riviera, from which one understands that he had to make a precipitate departure. Then he turned up in Berlin, and if our information is correct, Excellency, he was seen once or twice with Her Highness the Princess Elida. We have been asked quite unofficially whether we can give any information as to the nature of his activities."

"Well, you know the answer well enough," the Marchese replied irritably. "I have no knowledge of Major Fawley. Of my niece's acquaintances or companions I naturally can keep no count. If he is a suspected person, I regret her association with him, otherwise there is nothing to be said."

The young man took silent and respectful leave of his chief. The Ambassador, who was a very much worried man, lit a cigarette and studied the neatly typed list of his engagements for the next few days with a groan.

CHAPTER XIX

IT was the moment for the sake of which Elida had made many sacrifices. She had, for the first time in her life, disobeyed certain instructions issued from a beautiful white stone and marble building in the Plaza Corregio at Rome, instructions signed by the hand of a very great man indeed. Not only that, but, in quartering herself upon a relative whom she loved better than any other amongst her somewhat extensive family, she had involved him in many possible embarrassments. As she sat there she felt that she had offended against the code of her life, and, listening to the music in the far-away rooms, the hum of joyous voices, the passing backwards and forwards of men in brilliant uniforms and beautifully gowned women, she felt conscious of a sense of shame. Yet it all seemed worth while when young Hartley Stammers, second secretary at the American Embassy, the acquaintance of a few hours, from whom she had begged this favour, and Fawley, a quietly distinguished-looking figure in his plain evening clothes amongst this colourful gathering, suddenly appeared upon the threshold. The light which flashed for a single moment in his eyes filled her with a sort of painful joy. For the first time she felt weak of purpose. She was filled with a longing to abandon at that moment and for ever this stealthy groping through the tortuous ways of life, to respond instead to that momentary challenge with everything she had to give. Perhaps if the mask had not fallen quite so quickly she might have yielded.

"This is indeed a great pleasure, Princess," Fawley said courteously, as he raised her fingers to his lips. "I had no idea that you thought of coming to London."

"Nor I until—well, it seems only a few hours ago," she said. "My aunt has not been well and my uncle—you know him, I dare say—he is our Ambassador here—begged me to pay him a flying visit. So here I am! Arrived this evening. Will you not sit down, Major Fawley? I should like so much that we talk for a little time."

The younger man took regretful leave. Elida smiled at him delightfully. He had fulfilled a difficult mission and she was grateful.

"You will not forget, Mr. Stammers, that we dance later in the evening," she reminded him. "You must show me some of your new steps. None of our Italian men can dance like you Americans."

"I will be glad to," the boy promised a little ruefully. "I have a list of duty hops down here which makes me feel tired. I'll surely cut some of them if I can. Being sort of office boy of the place, they seem to leave me to do the cleaning up."

He took his leave, followed by Elida's benediction. The quiet place for which she had asked fulfilled all its purposes.

It was an alcove, as yet undiscovered by the majority of the guests, leading from one of the smaller refreshment-rooms. Fawley sank into the divan by her side.

"Why have you come to London?" he asked quietly.

"Is this bluntness part of the new diplomacy they talk about?" she retorted.

"It is the oldest weapon man has," he declared. "It is rather effective, you see, because it really demands a reply."

"What you really want to know," she reflected, "is whether I followed you."

"Something of the sort. Perhaps you may have had quite different ideas. I can assure you that so far as I am concerned——" He left the sentence unfinished. A very rare thing with him.

"I came here expressly to see you," she suddenly confessed. "It is quite important."

"You flatter me."

"You know all your people in Rome, of course?"

"Naturally. We Americans always know one another. We do not keep ourselves in water-tight compartments."

"Mr. Marston is a great friend of mine," she said. "Poor man, just now he seems so worried!"

"What? Jimmie Marston?" Fawley exclaimed. "That sounds quaint to me. I don't think I ever saw him when he did not look happy."

"He is what you call in your very expressive language a bluffer," she answered. "I know what the matter is with him now. He is terrified lest at any moment he may find himself in the imbroglio of a European war."

Like a flash the relaxation passed from Fawley's expression. His tone was unchanged, but he had relapsed into the stony-faced, polite, but casual guest performing his social duties.

"Our dear old friend," he observed, "is probably having an unfortunate love affair. He is the only one of our diplomats who has achieved the blue ribbon of the profession and remained a lover of women. They really ought not to have given him Rome. It was trying him too high."

"Yet not long ago," she reminded him, "you were pursuing your vocation there."

"Ah, but then I am not a lover of women," he declared.

"I wonder whether it matters," she went on. "I mean, I wonder whether outside the pages of the novelist Ambassadors ever do give away startling secrets to the Delilahs of my sex and whether they," she added, with a flash of her beautiful eyes, "ever win successes with a whisper which should cost them a lifetime's devotion."

With a murmured request for permission, he followed her example and lit a cigarette.

"One would like to believe in that sort of thing," he reflected, "but I do not think there is much of it nowadays. Whispers are too easily traced back, and if you once drop out of a profession it is terribly difficult to re-establish yourself. We Americans—you must have found that out for yourself—are an intensely practical people. We would not consider any woman in the world worth the loss of our career."

She leaned back in her corner of the divan and laughed melodiously.

"What gallantry!"

There was a certain return of good humour in his kindly smile.

"Let us be thankful, at any rate," he said, "that our relations are such that we do not need to borrow the one from the other."

Her fingers played nervously with her vanity-case.

"That may not last," she murmured, almost under her breath. "I did not follow you here for nothing."

He listened to the music.

"Rather a good tune?" he suggested.

She shook her head.

"Neither did I follow you here to dance with you."

He sighed regretfully.

"The worst of even the by-ways of my profession," he lamented, "is that duty so often interferes with pleasure. The Chief's wife, who, as I dare say you know, is my cousin, has given me a special list here, and I have to take the wife of the French Naval Attaché in to supper."

"I shall not keep you," she promised. "I should probably have sent you away before now if I had not felt reluctant to say what I came to say. Sit down for one moment and leave me when you please. It is necessary."

"Necessary?" he repeated.

She nodded. She was less at her ease than he had ever seen her. Her exquisite fingers were playing nervously with a jewel which hung from her neck.

"I think I told you once that I saw quite a good deal of your young brother in Rome during the hunting season."

"Micky?"

"Yes. The one in the Embassy. Third secretary, is he not?"

Fawley nodded.

"Well, what about him?"

"He is not quite so discreet as you are."

A queer silence. The sound of the music seemed to have faded away. When he spoke his voice was lower than ever, but there was an almost active belligerency in his tone.

"Just what do you mean?" he demanded.

"You are going to hate me, so get ready for it."

"For the first time in my life," he muttered, "I am inclined to wish that you were a man."

She was hardening a little. The first step was taken at any rate.

"Well, I am not, you see, and you can do nothing about it. Here is a scrappy note from your brother which I received a short time ago. It is written, as you see, on the Embassy notepaper."

She handed him an envelope. He drew out its contents deliberately and read the half-sheet of paper.

"*Dear Princess,*

"*I rather fancy that I am crazy but here you are. I send you copies of the last three code cables from Washington to the Chief. I have no access to the code and I cannot see what use they can be to you without it but I have kept my word.*

"*Don't forget our dance to-morrow night.*

"*Micky.*"

Fawley folded up the note and returned it.

"The copies of the various cables," she remarked, "were enclosed. Rather ingenuous of the boy, was it not, to imagine that anyone who interested themselves at all in the undercurrents of diplomacy had not the means of decoding despatches? They were all three very unimportant, though. They did not tell me what I wished to know."

There was a tired look in his eyes, but otherwise he remained impassive.

"Yes," he agreed, "it was ingenuous. It just shows that it is not quite fair to bring these lads fresh from college into a world where they meet women like you. Go on, please."

"The cables," she continued, "and your brother's note, if you wish for it, are at your disposal in return for accurate knowledge of just one thing."

"What is it you wish to know?" he asked.

"I wish to know why you came here to London instead of taking the information you collected in Germany straight to Rome."

"Anything else?"

"Whether Washington and London are likely to come to any agreement."

"Upon what?"

"Some great event which even the giants fear to whisper about."

"I have seldom," he declared, rising to his feet and beckoning to a young man who was standing upon the threshold of the ante-room looking in, "spent an hour in which the elements of humour and pleasure were so admirably blended. Dickson, young fellow, you are in luck," he went on, addressing the friend to whom he had signalled. "I am permitted to present you to the Princess di Vasena. Put your best foot foremost, and if you can dance as well as you used to, Heaven is about to open before you. Princess—to our next meeting."

He bowed unusually low and strolled away. She looked after him thoughtfully as she made room for the new-comer by her side.

"You were wondering?" the latter asked.

"When that meeting will be, for one thing. Major Fawley is always so mysterious. Shall we dance?"

CHAPTER XX

FAWLEY, during the course of his wanderings about the world, had years ago decided upon London as his head-quarters, and occupied in his hours of leisure a very delight-ful apartment in the Albany. At ten o'clock on the evening following the ball at Dorrington House a freckled young man, still in flying-clothes, was ushered into his room by the family servant whom he had brought with him from New York and established as caretaker.

"Mister Michael, sir," the latter announced. "Shall I serve dinner now?"

"Cocktails first," Fawley ordered, "then dinner as soon as you like. You won't need to change, Micky. Just get out of those ghoulish-looking clothes, have your bath and put on a dressing-gown or anything you like. That is, unless you want to go out. I am not moving myself this evening."

The young man appeared doubtful.

"The fact is, Martin, old chap," he confessed, "I have a very particular friend over in London just now. I thought of trying to see if I could locate her."

"The Princess di Vasena?" his brother enquired casually.

Micky stared at him.

"How the mischief did you guess?"

Fawley smiled a little sadly.

"This is not like home, you know, Micky. Here you have to picture to yourself nations and individuals all standing on tiptoe and crazy to get to know everybody else's business. The whole place is like a beastly whispering-gallery."

"Still, I don't see how——" the boy began with a puzzled frown.

"Go and get your bath and dry up," his brother interrupted. "I will send Jenkins round with a cocktail."

"Jove, that sounds good," Micky admitted. "I shan't be longer than twenty minutes. Awfully decent of you to wait dinner."

The cocktails tasted good, as indeed they were, for, granted the right material, the American touch on the shaker is after all the most subtle in the world. The dinner was excellent and the bottle of Pommery '14 iced to perfection was a dream. Michael Fawley, a rather loosely built but pleasant-looking lad, drew a deep sigh of content as he lit his pipe.

"Well, I don't know what you were in such a devil of a hurry to see me for, Martin, old chap," he observed, "but it is pretty well worth it even if they dock me the three days off my leave. French champagne tastes all wrong in Italy, and though the food is good enough for a time, it's monotonous—too many pâtés and knick-knacks for my taste. This is like New York, again."

"You always were fond of New York, weren't you, Micky?" his brother remarked speculatively.

"I'll say so," the boy assented. "New York and the summer life on Long Island should be good enough for anybody."

"I'm glad."

"What the devil do you mean?" Micky demanded, with a match hovering over the bowl of his pipe.

"I mean that I think you would be better out of this diplomatic business, young fellow," his brother said. "I want you to post your resignation to Washington to-night."

The match burnt out between the lad's fingers. He laid down his pipe and stared.

"For the love of Mike, what are you talking about, Martin?"

"You are too susceptible for our job, Micky," was the grave reply. "A little too credulous."

"Gee!" the young man muttered under his breath.

"I came across the Princess di Vasena last night," Fawley confided. "I am not going to say hard things about her, because, after all, I am in the same job myself, and if we take it on at all we have to go right through with it. It happens that there is something she wants very badly from me just now and she tried to bargain for it with a copy of those cables you sent her, Micky."

"Are you telling me," the boy cried in horror, "that the Princess di Vasena——"

"Come, come," Fawley interrupted. "Don't make such a tragedy of it, Micky. It isn't worth it. I could have told you directly I heard her name that you would have to be careful. She is in our Black Book, but of course that doesn't come round to the juniors. We don't think that they ought to know everything. There is no actual mischief done, I am glad to say, but that—to put it plainly—is not your fault."

Micky was petrified into a stark and paralysed silence. His hands were gripping the side of the table. He was ghastly pale. Fawley leaned over for a cigarette and lit it.

"There is just one rough word to be said, Micky," he continued, "and you can guess how I hate to say it, but it is better to get it over. You have offended against the code. You have to pay. It will be my business to see that no one knows anything about it, but you must post your resignation to Washington to-night and you must catch—let me see, I think it is the *Homeric*, the day after to-morrow for New York."

Micky picked up his pipe, relit it and smoked for a moment or two in silence. He came of good stock. He showed no signs of whimpering.

"You are dead right, Martin," he blundered out at last. "I cannot think how in hell I came to do it. It was not as though she vamped me, made any promises or that sort of thing. I was simply almighty crazy."

"Never mind, old chap," his brother remarked consolingly; "the thing is over and done with and so, perhaps fortunately, is your diplomatic career. You were not cut out for it. Fortunately those cables did not tell the Princess what she wanted to know. There is no real harm done—only a great principle broken. I hope we will see you over this side again, Micky, for the Walker Cup next year. You are a good lad, but I think you are better at golf than at diplomacy."

Micky walked over to the writing-table and drew out a sheet of paper.

"Dictate, Martin," he invited.

Fawley stood at the window looking out with his hands behind him. He knew precisely how much of his brother's composure was assumed, and he took care to keep his face averted.

"To Q.D.A.S. Department 137, Washington. Michael Fawley Third Secretary Rome begs leave tender resignation important family business stop confirmation by letter follows stop leave of absence already granted."

"Who has given me leave of absence?" the boy asked, looking up.

"Douglas Miller over here is able to deal with all these slight matters. Your Chief, as you know, is on the high seas. I told Miller what is quite true, that your family affairs at home were in the devil of a mess. You have far too much money, you know, Micky, like all of us, and he agreed to your getting out at once. There has not been a suspicion of anything else. There never will be unless you give it away yourself."

"And the Princess?" the boy faltered hopelessly. "Shan't I ever see her again?"

Fawley made no reply for the moment, then he swung slowly round in his chair. Micky, the personification of rather sulky boyhood, was leaning back on the divan with his hands in his pockets.

"How old are you, Micky?" he asked.

"Twenty-two."

"The Princess is thirty-two," Fawley confided. "There is nothing in the world to be said against her. She is noted throughout Europe as a woman of great charm and many accomplishments. She has, also, a little more brain than is good for her. I do not fancy that she has much use for boys, Micky, except when she can make use of them."

"Rubbing it in, aren't you?" the other muttered.

"For your own good, young fellow."

"I can look after myself," the boy grumbled.

"On Long Island, yes. At Newport, very likely. At any petting party at Bar Harbour I think you might be a star. But over here you are a trifle out of the game, Micky. We experienced ones have to don our armour when we come up against women like Elida."

"Hello!" Micky exclaimed. "Do you call her by her Christian name?"

"A slip of the tongue," Fawley confessed. "All the same, we have met quite a number of times lately. I don't mind telling you, Micky, in confidence, that she is the only woman who has ever tempted me to wish that I had never taken on my particular branch of work."

The younger man whistled softly. He was rather a cub in some matters, but he was honestly fond of his brother.

"Why don't you chuck it and marry her, then?" he asked.

Fawley smiled a little sadly.

"Mine is just one of those professions, Micky," he said, "which is pretty difficult to chuck. When you are once in it, you are in it for good or for evil. If you once leave the subterranean places and come out into the sunshine, there are risks. People do not forgive."

"Have you been looking for any particular sort of trouble, Martin?"

"Perhaps so. At any rate I have this consolation. The goal towards which I have been working for years is worth while. Any man in the world would feel justified in devoting his whole life, every energy of his brain, every drop of blood in his body, towards its accomplishment, yet I cannot even make up my own mind whether my last few months' energies have been the energies of an honourable man. I should hate to be arraigned at any Court in which my conscience would be the judge."

"That damned Quaker streak in our family cropping up," the young man muttered sympathetically.

"Perhaps so," his brother agreed. "After all, it is the old question of whether the end can justify the means. Soon I shall be face to face with the results which will tell me that; then I shall know whether I shall ever be able to rid myself of the fetters or not."

"I wonder," Micky speculated, "what makes you so eager to get out of harness. You were always the worker in our family."

"The same damned silly reason, I suppose, which has brought your diplomatic career to an end," Fawley answered with a note of savagery in his tone. "Within thirty seconds of knowing Elida di Vasena I saved her from committing a murder; within five minutes I had the evidence in my hand which would have sent her out to be shot as a spy; and within ten minutes I knew that I cared for her more than any other woman I have ever known."

"Does she know?" Micky asked, with a note of reverence in his tone.

"Was there ever a woman who did not know when she had succeeded in making a fool of a man?" Fawley rejoined bitterly. "I have not told her, if that is what you mean. I doubt whether I ever shall tell her."

Jenkins presented himself upon the threshold. He stood on one side as he opened the door.

"The Princess di Vasena, sir," he announced.

CHAPTER XXI

IT was evident from the moment of her entrance that Elida was not entirely her usual composed self. She was breathing rapidly as though she had run up the stairs. Her eyes darted restlessly round the room. The sight of Micky in no way discomposed her. She drew a sigh of relief as though the thing which she had feared to see was absent. She nodded to the young man as she held out her hand to Fawley.

"You see that my brother is here to answer for his sins," he remarked.

She sank into a chair.

"Poor Micky!" she exclaimed. "Some day I hope he will forgive me when he understands."

"Oh, I forgive you all right," Micky conceded. "I was just an ass. Didn't quite understand what I was doing, I suppose."

"Do any of us?" she lamented. "Please give me a cigarette, Martin. You have, perhaps, some brandy. I have been greatly disturbed and I am not well."

Fawley produced cigarettes, touched the bell and ordered the liqueur. Elida took one sip and set the glass down. She looked half fearfully at her host.

"The little girl of Krust—Greta—she has not been here?"

"Not that I know of," Fawley assured her. "I have not seen her since I left Berlin."

"Nor Krust? Nor Maurice von Thal?"

"Not one of them."

She seemed a trifle relieved. She threw open her cloak a little and tapped a cigarette upon the table. Her eyes were still full of trouble.

"I am almost afraid to ask my next question," she confessed. "Pietro Patoni?"

Fawley shook his head. This time he was bewildered but grave. If Patoni was in London, there might indeed be trouble.

"I have not seen him," he assured Elida, "since I was in Rome."

"I know the fellow," Micky put in. "Nephew of a holy cardinal, with eyes like beads. Looked like a cross between a stork and a penguin. Sort of fellow, if you were a Catholic you would cross yourself when you saw him and hope that you never met him again!"

Elida smiled despite her agitation.

"Kindly remember that he is my cousin," she said. "Anyhow, I am thankful that he has not found you out yet, Martin. I have word that he is in London, and if he is in London it is because he is looking for you. And if Krust is in London, or any of his emissaries, it is because they are looking for you. And if Greta and Nina are here, they are here for the same reason."

"Well, my name is in the directory," Fawley observed, "both here and in New York. I am perfectly easy to find. What do they want with me?"

"I think," Elida confided, "that they all want to kill you—especially Pietro."

"He looks just that sort of pleasant fellow," Fawley remarked.

"He hates all of us Americans," Micky grumbled. "He was never even decently civil to me."

Elida took another sip of her *fine*, lit a second cigarette and relaxed. A slight tinge of colour came into her cheeks. Her eyes had lost their tiredness.

"It is not so much that he hates Americans," she explained. "He resents their interference in European politics. He has a very clear idea of how the destinies of Italy should be shaped, and just now there are rumours passing across Europe which are stupefying everybody. I came over myself to see if I could learn anything of the truth. I am ashamed of what I did, but I wanted so much to know."

Her eyes were pleading with Fawley's. He avoided their direct challenge.

"To revert to this question of Prince Patoni and his antipathies," he said, "I should not think that America herself was very keen about any individual interference upon this side."

"Please do not try to mislead me any more," Elida begged. "I understand that I may not have your confidence—perhaps

I do not deserve it—but you need not try to throw dust in my eyes. There is something else I have to say."

She glanced at Micky and hesitated. He rose to his feet.

"I will be toddling off, Martin," he announced. "Good night, Princess."

"No ill-will, Mister Micky?" she asked, smiling. "Those cables were terribly uninteresting. They did me no good whatever."

He made a wry face.

"Sorry," he rejoined gruffly. "They didn't give me much of a boost!"

She waited patiently until the door was closed behind him, then she turned almost hysterically to Fawley.

"Why have you not reported to Berati?" she cried breathlessly. "Tell me what has brought you here. Do you know that you are in danger?"

"No, I don't think I realised that," he answered. "One always has to watch one's step, of course. I did not go back to Berati because I had not finished my job."

"What part of it have you to finish here in England?" she demanded.

"I had most of my clothes stolen in Berlin," he confided. "I had to come and visit my tailor."

"Is that sort of thing worth while with me?" she protested. "Do you not understand that I have come here to warn you?"

He smiled.

"This is London," he told her. "I am in sanctuary."

"Do you really believe that?" she asked wonderingly.

"Of course I do."

Elida shook her head. She seemed very tired. There was a note of despair in her tone.

"That man Berati is always right," she lamented. "He told me that the ideal Secret Service man or woman did not exist. They are all either too brave or too cowardly. If you have no fear, you have no caution. If you have no caution, you are to be caught by the heels. Very well. For you, perhaps, that may be nothing—life must end with all of us, but for your work it is finality. The knowledge you have acquired is lost. You are a failure."

"You really have a great gift of intelligence, Elida," Fawley declared, in a non-committal tone.

"It does not amount to intelligence," she objected. "It is common sense. Very well. Let us continue. You think that you are safe in London, when you have failed to report to Berati, when there are rumours going about in Rome that you are not to be trusted, that you have all the time been working for a cause of your own concerning which no one knows anything. Italy has sent over her spies. They are here now. In Germany they have the same distrust. Krust has given word that you are to be removed, and Krust has more assassins at his back than any man in the world. Maurice von Thal swore only three nights ago that this next time he would not fail. Even Behrling has doubts of you! In France it is almost as bad. They suspect you of double espionage and of selling some great secret of theirs of which even I know nothing."

"It all sounds very unpleasant," Fawley murmured under his breath.

She took a cigarette from the box. Her slim, beautiful fingers were shaking so that she lit it with difficulty. Fawley bent over her and steadied her hand. She looked up at him pathetically.

"Now I shall qualify for the executioner's bullet," she went on. "There is one of Berati's spies outside on the pavement at the present moment. Another one has applied for a position as valet in this building. I do not say that either of these men has instructions to proceed to extremes. I do not know. This I do know. They are to keep a faithful record of your movements hour by hour and minute by minute. Patoni, on the other hand, scoffs at such mildness. He, like Maurice, has sworn to kill you on sight. Krust's men have the same instructions, and they are clever—diabolically clever. You will see that the situation is not wholly agreeable, my friend."

"It certainly is not," was the grim reply.

"So now again I ask you," Elida continued, "what are you doing in London, Martin, when you should be in Rome? You acquired a great deal of information in Berlin which Berati needs. You are his man. What are you doing in London?"

"That I cannot tell you just yet," Fawley said gravely. "But, Elida, believe me when I tell you that I am not working for the harm of Italy or Germany or France. I may not have kept my word to the letter with any one of these countries, or rather with their representatives to whom I have talked, but I have been aiming at great things. If the great things come, it does not matter what happens to me. And they may come. In the meantime I can do so little. A single false movement and calamity might follow."

"You speak in riddles," Elida faltered, "but I trust you, Martin. None of the others do. I trust you, dear Martin. If I could help—if I could save you—I would give my life!"

For a moment he took her lightly and reverently, yet with a faint touch of the lover, into his arms. The worn look passed from her face. Her eyes suddenly lost their terrified gleam, a tremor of joy seemed to pass through her body. He drew quietly away, but he kept her hand in his.

"Tell me," he asked, "are you here officially?"

She shook her head.

"They do not trust me any more," she confided.

"Then why are you here?" he persisted.

She lifted her eyes. Since those last few minutes they were so soft and sweet, so full of expression, that at that moment she was entirely and utterly convincing.

"Because I am such a big fool. Because I like to see you. Because I knew that you were in danger on every side. I had to tell you. You must have thought me such an ordinary little adventuress," she said wistfully. "You will forgive me for that? All that I wanted to know I wanted to know for your sake—that I might help you——"

The door was suddenly half flung, half kicked open. Micky, in his pyjamas, swayed upon the threshold. All his fresh colour had gone. He was gripping the wainscoting as though for support. There was an ugly splash of colour on his chest.

"Fellow in your room, Martin," he faltered. "Room—Jenkins told me I was to sleep. Must have been—hiding somewhere."

Fawley half carried, half dragged his brother to a couch. Elida sprang to the bell and kept her finger upon it.

"Did you see the fellow, Micky?" Fawley asked.

"Looked like a foreigner. He came out from behind the wardrobe—only a few feet away—and shot at me just as I was getting into bed."

Fawley gave swift orders to Jenkins, who was already in the room. Elida had possessed herself of a shirt and was making a bandage.

"There will be a doctor here in a minute, Micky," his brother said. "Close your eyes. I must have a look. Elida is there making a bandage for you. Missed your heart by a thirtieth of an inch, thank God," he went on. "Don't faint, old chap. I can't give you a drink, but I am going to rub some brandy on your lips. God, what a fool I was to let you sleep in my room!"

"An undersized little rat," Micky gasped, with feeble indignation. "I could have squeezed the life out of him if he'd given me the chance. He turned out the lights and stole up behind. What are you in trouble with the Dagos for, Martin?"

"You think he was a Dago, then?"

"Sure. What about the police?"

Fawley shook his head.

"We ought to send for them, I suppose, but it is not altogether etiquette in the profession."

"Am I in on one of your jobs, then, Martin?" the boy asked with a weak grin.

"Looks like it," his brother assented. "I'm damned sorry. It was Jenkins's fault putting you in there. You were not prepared, of course."

"Well, I didn't think it was necessary to hold a gun in your right hand and untie your tie with the left in London," Micky grumbled. "I have done something like that in Chicago."

Then the door swung open. The man with the bald head, the beady eyes and the long jaw stood upon the threshold. He seemed to grasp the situation in a moment. With an impatient turn of the shoulder he threw back the long evening cape he was wearing. His hand flashed out just too late. He was looking into the muzzle of Fawley's steadily held and vicious-looking revolver.

"That won't do here, Patoni," the latter said in a voice such as no one in the room had ever heard him use before. "Drop your gun. Before I count three, mind. There's going to be none of that sort of thing. One—two——"

Patoni's weapon fell smoothly on to the carpet. Fawley kicked it towards Elida, who stooped and picked it up. From outside they heard the rattle of the lift.

"That's the doctor," Fawley announced. "Micky, can you get back to your room? You will find Jenkins there to help you."

"I guess so," the young man replied, moving unsteadily towards the door.

"An accident, remember," Fawley continued. "You were unpacking your gun and it went off—shaking a cartridge out or anything you like. The doctor won't be too particular. He leaves that sort of thing to the police, and we don't want the police in on this."

There were hurried footsteps outside and the door was thrown open. Jenkins was there, the doctor, the liftman. Micky staggered towards them.

"Take Mr. Michael into my room, Jenkins," Fawley ordered. "Let the doctor examine him there and report. I have looked at the wound. I do not think it is dangerous. Close the door and leave us."

Fawley's voice was not unduly raised, but some quality in it seemed to compel obedience. They all disappeared. Elida, obeying a gesture from him, closed the door. He pointed to a chair.

"Sit down, Prince," he directed.

CHAPTER XXII

FAWLEY, gentle though he was in his methods, was running no risks. He seated himself at his desk, his revolver lying within a few inches of his fingers. Patoni was a yard or so away towards the middle of the room. Elida was on Fawley's left.

"What do you want with me, Prince Patoni?" Fawley asked.

The Italian's eyes were full of smouldering anger.

"A great deal," he answered. "General Berati has sent me here with an order which I have in my pocket—you can see it when you choose—that you accompany me at once to Rome. Furthermore, I am here to know what my cousin the Princess Elida is doing in London, and particularly what she is doing in your room at this hour of the night."

"That is my own affair entirely," Elida declared. "He is an impertinent fellow, this cousin of mine," she went on, turning to Fawley. "He follows me about. He persecutes me. In Rome it is not permitted. There are too many of my own people there. I have a brother if I need a protector."

"Is it not true," he demanded, "that you were once engaged to me?"

"For four days," she answered. "Then I discovered that I hated your type. Proceed with your business with Major Fawley. Leave me out of it, if you please."

Patoni's eyes flamed for a moment with malignant fire. He turned his shoulder upon her and faced Fawley. For the moment he had lost his guise of the Cardinal's nephew, the politician's secretary. His rasping tone, his drawn-up frame, once more recalled the cavalry officer.

"I have told you, Major Fawley," he said, "that I have in my pocket an order from General Berati requiring your immediate presence in Rome. I have an aeroplane waiting at Heston now. I should be glad to know whether it would be convenient for you to leave at dawn."

"Most inconvenient," Fawley answered. "Besides, I hate the early-morning air. Why does the General want me before my work is finished?"

"He demands to know what part of the work he entrusted you with concerns England?"

"He will find that easy to understand later on," was the smooth rejoinder.

"I am not talking about later on," Patoni declared harshly. "I am talking about now. I represent General Berati. You can see my mandate if you will. I am your chief. What are you doing in England when you should have taken the information you gained in Berlin direct to Rome?"

"Working still for the good of your country," Fawley assured him.

"No one has asked you to work independently for the good of our country," was the swift retort. "You have been asked to obey orders, to study certain things and report on them. Not one of these concerns England. You are not supposed to employ any initiative. You are supposed to work to orders."

"I must have misunderstood the position," Fawley observed. "I never work in that way. I preserve my own independence always. Was Berati not satisfied with me for my work on the frontier?"

"It was fine work," Patoni admitted grudgingly. "To show you that I am not prejudiced, I will tell you something. Five men we have sent one after the other to check the details of your work, to confirm the startling information you submitted as to the calibre of the anti-aircraft guns, and to report further upon the object of the subterranean work which has been carried to our side of the frontier. One by one they disappeared. Not one of the five has returned alive!"

"It was murder to send them," Fawley remarked. "I do not say that they might not have done as well as I did if they had been the first, but unfortunately I did not get clean away, and after that the French garrison redoubled their guards."

"The matter of the frontier is finished and done with," Patoni declared. "I have no wish to sit here talking. Here are the General's instructions."

He drew a paper from his pocket and smoothed it out in front of Fawley. The latter glanced at it and pushed it away.

"Quite all right, beyond a doubt," he admitted. "The only thing is that I am not coming with you."

"You refuse?" Patoni demanded, his voice shaking with anger.

"I refuse," Fawley reiterated. "I am a nervous man and I have learnt to take care of myself. When you introduce yourself into my apartment following close upon an attempt at assassination by one of your countrymen, I find myself disinclined to remain alone in your company during that lonely flight over the Alps, or anywhere else, in fact."

"This will mean trouble," Patoni warned him.

"What more serious trouble can it mean," Fawley asked, "than that you should commence your mission to me—if ever you had one—by having one of your myrmidons steal into my bedroom and nearly murder my brother, who was unfortunately occupying it in my place? That is a matter which has to be dealt with between you and me, Patoni."

The Italian's right hand groped for a minute to the spot where the hilt of his sword might have been.

"That is a private affair," he said. "I am ready to deal with it at any time. I am a Patoni and we are in the direct line with the di Rezcos. The presence of my cousin in your rooms is a matter to be dealt with at once."

"It will be dealt with by ordering you out of them," Fawley retorted, as he pressed the bell.

Patoni sprang to his feet. He looked more than ever like some long, lean bird of prey.

"This is an insult!" he exclaimed.

Elida rose from her chair and moved over between the two men. It was her cousin whom she addressed.

"No brawling in my presence, if you please," she insisted. "You have put yourself hopelessly in the wrong, Pietro. A would-be assassin cannot claim to be treated as a man of honour."

"A would-be assassin!" he exclaimed furiously.

"I will repeat the words if you choose," she went on coldly. "I, too, am well served by my entourage. I know quite well that you arrived in this country with two members of Berati's guard, and that it was you yourself who gave the orders for the attack upon Major Fawley."

"You are a traitress!" he declared.

"You may think what you will of me," she rejoined, "so long as you leave me alone."

"Am I to suffer the indignity, then, of finding you here alone with this American at this hour of the night?" Patoni demanded harshly.

"So far as you are concerned there is no indignity," Elida replied. "You are not concerned. I am past the age of duennas. I do as I choose."

Jenkins presented himself in answer to the bell.

"Show this gentleman out," his master instructed.

The man bowed and stood by the opened door. Patoni turned to his cousin.

"You will leave with me, Elida."

She shook her head.

"I shall leave when I am ready, and I shall choose my own escort," she replied. "It will not be you!"

Patoni was very still and very quiet. He moved a few steps towards the door. Then he turned round.

"I shall report to my Chief what I have seen and heard," he announced. "I think that it will cure him of employing any more mercenaries in the affairs of our country."

"I hope that at the same time he will be cured of sending offensive envoys," Fawley concluded, with a valedictory wave of the hand.

CHAPTER XXIII

THE Right Honourable Willoughby Johns, the very harassed British Minister, fitted on a pair of horn-rimmed spectacles and studied the atlas which lay before him.

"Take a sharp pencil, Malcolm," he invited his secretary, "and trace the frontier for me from the sea upwards."

The latter promptly obeyed. The map was one which had been compiled in sections, and the particular one now spread out stretched from Nice to Bordighera.

"You will find it a little irregular, sir," he warned his chief. "The road from the sea here mounts to the official building on the main thoroughfare in a fairly straight line, but after that in the mountains it becomes very complicated. This will doubtless be the excuse the French authorities will offer in the matter of the subterranean passages."

"And the roads?"

"There is a first-class road on the French side from a place called Sospel running in this direction, sir. The whole range of hills on the right-hand side is strongly fortified, but our military report which I was studying this afternoon at the War Office with General Burns still gives the situation here entirely in favour of an attacking force. Fawley's latest information, however," the secretary went on, dropping his voice, "changes the situation entirely. The new French defences starting from this bulge here, and which comprise some of the finest subterranean work known, strike boldly across the frontier and now command all the slopes likely to be dangerous. If a copy of Fawley's plan should reach Italy, I imagine that there would be war within twenty-four hours."

"Has Fawley reported any fresh movements of troops in the neighbourhood?"

"Major Fawley himself, as you know, sir, has been in Berlin for some short time," Malcolm replied. "So far as our ordinary sources of information are concerned, we gather that everything on the Italian side is extraordinarily quiet. The French, on the other hand, have been replacing a lot of their five-year-old guns with new Creuzots at the places marked, and trains with locked wagons have been passing through Cagnes, where we have had a man stationed every hour through the night for very nearly a fortnight. So far as we know, however, there has been no large concentration of troops."

The Prime Minister studied the atlas for some minutes and then pushed it on one side.

"Seems to me there is some mystery about all this," he observed. "Bring me Grey's textbook upon Monaco."

"I have it in my pocket, sir," the young man confided, producing the small volume. "You will see that the French have practically blotted out Monaco as an independent State. There is no doubt that they will treat the territory in any way they wish. The old barracks at the top of Mont Agel, which used to contain quite a formidable number of men and a certain strength in field artillery, have been evacuated and everything has been pushed forward towards the frontier. It would seem that the whole military scheme of defence has been changed."

The Prime Minister leaned back in his chair a little wearily.

"Telephone over to the War Office and see if General Burns is still there," he directed. "Say I should like to see him."

"Very good, sir. Is there anything more I can do?"

"Not at present. The call to Washington is through, I suppose?"

"You should be connected in half an hour, sir."

"Very well. Send in General Burns the moment he arrives."

Henry Malcolm, the doyen of private secretaries, took his leave. For another twenty minutes the Prime Minister studied the atlas with its pencilled annotations and the pile of memoranda which had been left upon his desk. A queer, startling situation! No one could make out quite what it meant. Willoughby Johns, as he pored over the mass of miscellaneous detail which had been streaming in for the last forty-eight hours, was inclined to wonder whether after all there was anything in it. Another war at a moment's notice! The idea seemed idiotic. He took a turn or two up and down the room with its worn but comfortable furniture, its spacious, well-filled book-shelves. His familiar environment seemed in some way a tonic against these sinister portents.... There was a tap at the door. Malcolm presented himself once more.

"General Burns was at the Foreign Office, sir," he announced. "He will be round in five minutes."

The Prime Minister nodded. He glanced at his watch. Still only seven o'clock. A telephone message from Washington to wait for, and he had been up at six. He listened to the subdued roar of traffic in the Buckingham Palace Road and the honking of taxis in the Park. Men going home after their day's work, without a doubt, home to their wives and children. Or calling perhaps at the club for a cheerful rubber of bridge and a whisky and soda. What a life! What peace and rest for harassed nerves! Dash it all, he would have a whisky and soda himself! He rang the bell twice. A solemn but sympathetic-looking butler presented himself.

"Philpott," his master ordered, "whisky and soda—some of the best whisky you have—and Schweppe's soda-water—no siphons."

"Very good, sir," the man replied, rather startled. "Would you care for a biscuit as well, sir?"

"Certainly. Two or three biscuits."

"Mr. Malcolm was saying that you had cancelled the dinner with the Cordonas Company to-night, sir."

"Quite right," Willoughby Johns assented. "No time for public dinners just now. I will have something here later on after the call from Washington has been through."

The man took his departure only to make very prompt reappearance. The whisky and soda was excellent. The Prime Minister drank it slowly and appreciatively. He made up his mind that he would have one every night at this hour. He hated tea. It was many hours since lunch, at which he had drunk one glass of light hock. Of course he needed sustenance. All the doctors, too, just now were preaching alcohol, including his own. Nevertheless, he felt a little guilty when General Burns was ushered in.

"Come in, General," he welcomed him. "Glad I caught you. Take a chair."

Burns, the almost typical soldier, a man of quick movements and brusque speech, took the chair to which he was motioned.

"My time is always at your disposal, sir," he said. "I very seldom leave before nine anyway."

The Prime Minister crumpled up his last piece of biscuit and swallowed it, finished his whisky and soda and stretched himself out with the air of a man refreshed.

"What is all this trouble down south, Burns?" he asked.

The General smiled sardonically.

"We leave it to you others to discover that, sir," he replied. "We only pass on the externals to you. I don't like the look of things myself, but there may be nothing in it."

"You started the scare," the Prime Minister reminded him reproachfully.

"I beg your pardon, sir, I would not call it that," the other protested. "What I did was to send in a report to the Foreign Office, as it was my duty to do, that there were at the present moment in Monte Carlo and Nice a larger number of Secret Service men of various nationalities than I have ever known drawn towards one spot since 1914."

"Who are they? Is there any report of their activities further than these formal chits and despatches?" Willoughby Johns asked.

"They scarcely exist by name, sir. There have been seven men from the eastern section of the newly established Italian Secret Service staying in Monte Carlo at once. They mingled freely with everyone and gambled at the tables, but recently five of them are said to have disappeared completely. There have been various reports about them, but nothing authentic."

"What do you imagine yourself has happened to them?" the Prime Minister enquired.

The General shrugged his shoulders.

"My opinion, sir, is," he said, "that they got lost in the mountains and fell into the hands of people who have an ugly way with strangers. They take their risks, of course, but no one has complained. Then there is a Frenchman there, Marquet. One of the cleverest agents who ever breathed. He sits in an easy-chair in the Hôtel de France lounge practically the whole of the day, but somehow or other he gets to know things. Then there were two Germans—Krust, the great industrialist, who is supposed to be a supporter of the Crown Prince, and another one whom I do not know. We have our own two men; one of them has a villa and never leaves Monte Carlo, and the other resides in Nice. Finally, if I may mention his name, there is the American, Major Fawley, who is reported to have been drowned at the entrance to the harbour, but whom we have heard of since in Germany. He would be a useful man to talk to if we could get hold of him."

"Ah, yes, Major Fawley," the Prime Minister reflected.

"Fawley's report about affairs in Berlin, if he ever got there, would be extraordinarily interesting," the General remarked.

The Prime Minister looked vague.

"I thought it was one of the peculiarities of the man," he observed, "that he never made reports."

"He is a remarkable traveller. One meets him in the most unexpected places. He believes in *viva-voce* reports."

The Prime Minister stroked his chin.

"I suppose you know that he is in London, Burns?" he asked.

"Only half an hour ago. We were not, as a matter of fact, looking out for him. We were interested in the wanderings of the Princess di Vasena, and we tracked her down to Major Fawley's rooms at the Albany."

"Your men are good workers," the Prime Minister approved.

"Espionage in London is easy enough. You must appreciate the fact, though, sir, that to have a man like Fawley working outside the department, who insists upon maintaining this isolation, makes it rather difficult for us."

"That is all very well, General," the Prime Minister declared impatiently. "Personally I hate Secret Service work, but we have to make use of it. We are up against the gravest of problems. No one can make out what is going on in Rome or in Berlin. We are compelled to employ every source of information. Fawley is invaluable to us, but you know the situation. We are under great obligations to him and he has done as much, without the slightest reward or encouragement, to bring about a mutual understanding between Washington and Downing Street as was possible for any human being. He works for the love of the work. He will accept no form of reward. All that he asks is freedom from surveillance so that he can work in his own fashion. I admit that the position must seem strange to you others, but I am afraid that we cannot alter it."

The General rose thoughtfully to his feet. The Prime Minister, whose nerves were a little on edge, waved him back again.

"It is no good taking this matter the wrong way, Burns," he said. "We are having far more trouble with M.2.XX. at

Scotland Yard than with you. There was a fight of some sort in Major Fawley's rooms at the Albany last night. His young brother got rather badly wounded. Fawley simply insists upon it that the whole affair is hushed up, yet we know that in that room were the Princess Elida di Vasena, Prince Patoni, her cousin—the private secretary of Berati, mark you—and Fawley. To add to the complication the young man, who was Third Secretary at Rome, has resigned from the service and is going back to New York to-morrow if he is well enough to travel. The Sub-Commissioner is furious with the Home Secretary, and the Home Secretary complains to us. Nothing matters. We have given our word to Fawley and we have to keep it."

"Why?" the General asked calmly.

The Prime Minister smiled.

"I don't blame you for asking that question, General," he went on, "and I will give you an honest reply. Because I myself and the two others who have to bear the brunt of affairs during these days of fierce anxiety have come to one definite conclusion. Fawley is the only man in Europe to-day who can save us from war."

Malcolm made hurried entrance.

"The call to Washington is through, sir, in your private cabinet," he announced.

General Burns saluted and took his leave. The Prime Minister hurried to the telephone.

It was ten minutes later when a furious ringing of the bell in the small room sent Malcolm hurrying in to his chief. The Prime Minister was restlessly pacing up and down the room. There seemed to be new lines in his face. He was haggard as though with a sense of fresh responsibilities. Yet with it all there was a glow of exaltation. He was like a man in the grip of mighty thoughts. He looked at Malcolm for a moment, as the latter entered the room and closed the door behind him, almost vaguely.

"You have spoken to Washington, sir?"

The Prime Minister nodded.

"Malcolm," he instructed his secretary, "I want Fawley here within half an hour."

"Fawley, sir?" the young man repeated anxiously. "But you know our agreement? As a matter of fact the house is being watched at this minute. London seems to have become as full of spies as any place on the Continent could be. Would it not be best, sir——"

"I must see Fawley myself and at once," the Prime Minister said firmly. "If an armed escort is necessary, provide it. Do you think that you can find him?"

"There will be no difficulty about that, sir," the young man replied doubtfully. "He keeps us informed of his movements from hour to hour. If this Prince Patoni, the envoy from Italy, discovers that Fawley is in direct communication with you, though, sir, it might lead to any sort of trouble," Malcolm said gravely.

"It is worth the risk," was the dogged reply. "Have a squad of police if you want them and clear the street. Anderson will see to that for you. Fawley can arrive as an ordinary dinner guest in a taxicab, but whatever happens, Fawley must come."

"It shall be arranged, sir," Malcolm promised.

CHAPTER XXIV

AFTER all, it seemed as though a great deal of fuss had been made about nothing. There were certainly half a dozen curious strollers in Downing Street, but the small cordon of policemen around the entrance to Number Ten awakened no more than ordinary comment. People of international importance were passing through those portals by day and by night, and in these disturbed times an escort was not unusual. Fawley himself, dressed in the Clubman's easy garb of short jacket and black tie, with a black slouch hat pulled over his eyes and a scarf around his throat, was quite unrecognisable as he jumped lightly from the taxi, passed the fare up to the driver, and stepped swiftly across the pavement and through the already opened door. He was ushered at once into Malcolm's room. The two men, who were old friends, shook hands.

"Any idea what's wrong?" Fawley asked.

"Very likely nothing at all," Malcolm replied. "I have spoken to Washington twice to-day and I gathered there was something stirring in our Department. They wanted the Prime Minister himself at seven o'clock. The Chief spoke and came out from the box looking rather like a man who had had a shock, and yet who had found something exciting at the back of it all. He insisted upon breaking all rules and seeing you here himself at once. I hope you did not mind the cavalcade. It was my job to get you here safely at all costs."

"I generally find I am safer alone," Fawley confided, "but I didn't mind at all. The others dropped out at the corner of the street and made a sort of semi-circular drive down. Queer days we are living in, Malcolm."

There was a knock at the door. The butler entered.

"The Prime Minister asks if you have dined, sir," he said, addressing Fawley. "If not, will you join him in a simple dinner in ten minutes?"

"Delighted," Fawley assented.

"I was to ask you to entertain Major Fawley for that time, sir," the man went on, turning to Malcolm.

"You and I will do the entertaining together, Philpott," the secretary replied with a smile.

"Dry Martinis, sir?" the man asked.

"A couple each and strong," Malcolm specified. "This has been a wearing day. And bring some more cigarettes, Philpott."

"This sounds like good news," Fawley remarked, installing himself in an armchair. "The cocktails, I mean. Any late news from Berlin?"

"We had a message through half an hour ago," Malcolm confided. "The city is still in a turmoil, but Behrling seems to have got them going. I think the Chief hit it on the nail at the luncheon to-day when he remarked that he could not make up his mind whether a weak and disrupted Germany for a time or a strong and united country gave us the best hope of peace."

Fawley sipped his cocktail appreciatively. He made no comment on the other's remarks. Just at the moment he had nothing to say about Germany even to the secretary of the British Prime Minister.

"Good show at the American Embassy last night," he observed.

"I didn't go," Malcolm regretted. "The Chief just now is too restless for me to get away anywhere and feel comfortable. I cannot help feeling that there is something of terrific importance in the air, of which even I know nothing."

The two men smoked on for a minute or two in silence. Then Fawley asked his host a question.

"Are those fellows outside waiting to ride home with me?"

"I'm afraid so," Malcolm assented. "You see, the Chief gave special orders to M.I.2, and they brought Scotland Yard into it. We know how you hate it, but the Chief is just as obstinate, and it seems you must be kept alive at all hazards for the next week or so."

"They didn't stop a mad Italian having a go at me last night," Fawley grumbled. "Got my brother instead. Not much harm done, I'm glad to say. What sort of an Italian colony is yours here?"

"No idea," Malcolm confessed. "This sort of work that you go in for is right outside my line. From what I have heard, though, I believe they are a pretty tough lot. Not as bad as in your country, though."

"They don't need to be," Fawley smiled. "As a rule I find it pretty easy to slip about, but it seems I am not popular in Rome just now."

"These fellows to-night didn't annoy you in any way, I hope?" Malcolm asked.

"Not in the least. I dare say, as a matter of fact, they were very useful. I don't take much notice of threats as a rule, but I had word on the telephone that they were laying for me."

"Official?"

"I think not. I think it was a private warning."

The butler re-opened the door.

"The Prime Minister is down, sir," he announced. "If you will allow me, I will show you the way to the small dining-room."

"See you later," Malcolm observed.

"I hope so," Fawley answered. "By the by, I shan't be sorry to have you keep those fellows to-night, Malcolm. First time in my life I've felt resigned to having nursemaids in attendance, but there is a spot of trouble about."

Malcolm's forehead wrinkled in surprise. He had known Fawley several years, but this was the first time he had ever heard him utter any apprehension of the sort.

"I'll pass word along to the sergeant," he promised. "They would not have been going in any case, though, until they had seen you safely home...."

Fawley had the rare honour of dining alone with the Prime Minister. As between two men of the world their conversation could scarcely be called brilliant, but, when dinner was over and at the host's orders coffee and port simultaneously placed upon the table, the Prime Minister unburdened himself.

"You are a man of experience, Fawley," he began. "You would call things on the Continent pretty critical, wouldn't you?"

"Never more so," Fawley assented. "If any one of five men whom Italy sent out to the frontier had got back to Rome alive there would have been war at the present moment."

The Prime Minister was allowing himself a glass of port and he sipped it thoughtfully.

"It's a funny thing," he went on. "We have ambassadors in every country of Europe and they keep making reports to us which are of great interest. When anything goes wrong, however, they are always the most surprised men in the world."

"You must remember," Fawley pointed out, "they are not allowed a Secret Service Department. The last person to hear of trouble as a rule is, as you say, the ambassador to the country concerned. What can you do about it, though?"

"Not much, I'm afraid," the other sighed. "Take our friend at Rome. It was only last night we had a long rigmarole from the Embassy there. The ambassador said he had never been more deeply impressed with the earnest desire of a certain great man for European peace. All the time we know that Berati has the draft of a treaty ready for the signature of whichever party in Germany comes out on top."

"Berati very nearly made a mistake there," Fawley remarked. "Still, I don't know that he was to be blamed. There were a few hours when I was in Berlin when the chances were all in favour of a monarchy. Von Salzenburg and his puppet played the game badly, or they would have won all right."

"Shall I tell you why I sent for you to-night?" the Prime Minister asked abruptly.

"I wish you would," was the very truthful and earnest response.

"You have your finger upon the situation in Germany and in Rome. You are not so well informed about the Quai d'Orsay, perhaps, but you know something about that. You know that war is simmering. Can you think of any means by which trouble can be postponed for, say, one week?"

"You mean," Fawley said, "keep things as they are for a week?"

"Yes."

"And after that week?"

"Rawson is on his way over. He is coming on the new fast liner and there is a question of sending a plane to meet him. You know what this means, Fawley."

"My God!"

There was a brief and curious silence. Fawley, the man of unchanging expression, the man whose thoughts no one could ever divine, was suddenly agitated. The light of the visionary so often somnolent in his eyes was back again. His face was transfigured. He was like a prophet who has suddenly been given a glimpse of the Heaven he has preached. . . . The Prime Minister was a man of impulses. He leaned over and laid his hand in friendly fashion for a moment on the other's shoulder.

"I know what this must mean to you, Fawley," he said. "The long and short of it is—so far as I could gather—the President is coming in. He is going to adopt your scheme. What we have to do now is to keep things going until Rawson arrives."

"How much of this can be told to—say—three men in Europe?" Fawley asked.

"I have thought of that," the Prime Minister replied. "You know that I am not an optimist—I have been coupled with the Gloomy Dean before now—yet I tell you that from a single word the President let fall this evening, they have made up their minds. America is going to make a great sacrifice. She is going to depart from her principles. She is going to join hands with us. It will be the launching of your scheme, Fawley.... Don't think that your labours are over, though. It is up to you to stop trouble until Rawson arrives. On that day we shall communicate simultaneously with France, Italy and Germany. Until that day what has to be done must be done unofficially."

"It shall be done," Fawley swore. "A week ago I heard from the White House. They were still hesitating."

"They only came to an agreement this morning," the Prime Minister announced. "It was the recent happenings in Germany which decided them. Another Hohenzollern régime—even the dimmest prospect of it—was enough to set the greatest democratic country in the world shivering."

"It shall be done," Fawley repeated stubbornly, and the light was flaming once more in his eyes. "For one week I shall be free from all the bullets in the world."

"I shall ask you nothing of your plans," the Prime Minister continued. "In years to come—on my death-bed, I think—these few minutes we are spending together will be one of the great memories of my life.... I have been reading my history lately. It is not the first time that the future of the world has been changed by subterranean workings."

"You can call me a spy if you like," Fawley observed with a smile. "I don't mind."

"You shouldn't mind," the Prime Minister replied. "They tell me that you are a millionaire, and I know myself that you accept no decoration or honours except from your own country. What a reward, though, your own conscience will bring you if we succeed! Think of the millions of lives that will be saved and lived out to their natural end. Think of the great sum of unhappiness which will be avoided—the broken hearts of the women, the ugliness of a ruined and blasted world. Fawley, sometimes the thought of another war and one's responsibilities concerning it comes to me like a hideous nightmare. Twice I have suffered from what they call a nervous breakdown. It was from the fear that war might come again in my days. Think of being in your place!"

Fawley rose to his feet. "I shall be no more than a cog in the wheels, sir," he sighed. "I just had the idea. Directly it has been put on paper, the sheer simplicity of it will amaze everyone. I am going to gamble on Rawson."

"I will back you," the Prime Minister declared. "I tell you I know for a certainty that he brings the President's signature."

Fawley glanced at the clock.

"Very good, sir," he said. "Will you allow me to arrange with Malcolm for the most powerful Government plane that can be spared? I shall want it ready at Heston tomorrow morning at six o'clock."

"Where are you off to first?"

"I am afraid I shall have to go to Paris, where I am not very popular; and on to Rome, where they have sworn to have my blood. Something I saw in Germany, though, will help me there. If my scheme comes off, there will be no war."

The Prime Minister held out both his hands. Afterwards he took his guest by the arm.

"We will go in to Malcolm together, Fawley," he proposed. "Paris and Rome, eh? And Germany afterwards. Well, you are a brave man."

CHAPTER XXV

FAWLEY, with his hands thrust into his overcoat pockets and a freshly lit cigarette in his mouth, walked briskly to the corner of Downing Street and paused, looking around for a taxicab, apparently unconscious that he was the cynosure of a dozen pairs of eyes. A private car was waiting by the side of the kerbstone to all appearance unoccupied. Suddenly he felt a grip upon his arm—not the sinister grip of an assailant, but the friendly grasp of slender fingers.

"Do not hesitate for one moment, please," the slim figure by his side insisted. "Step into that car."

He looked down at her with a smile. He knew very well that he had nothing to fear, for there were shadowy figures hovering around close at hand.

"Am I to be abducted again, Princess?" he asked. "This time I warn you that I have protectors at my elbow."

"It is nevertheless I," she declared a little petulantly, "who have to be your protector-in-chief. You do such foolish things—you who are on the black list of two countries, both of whom are well known for the efficiency of their Secret Service, and you walk about these streets as though you were invisible!"

He smiled, but he followed her obediently into the car. One of those shadowy figures stepped into the roadway and whispered a word to the driver. Elida gave the man the address of the Italian Embassy.

"Alas! I must get back to my rooms," he told her. "Sorry, but it is really important."

"You will come out from them on a stretcher if you do," she answered. "Honestly, I sometimes cannot decide whether you are wilfully stupid or whether you have that sort of courage which marches with luck."

"What have I to fear at my rooms?" he asked. "I can assure you that there will be no strangers allowed in the building for a long time to come."

"The man whom you have to fear is Pietro Patoni," she replied firmly. "I tell you this seriously, not as a fashion of speech. He has gone mad! I am sure of it. He believes—oh, I cannot tell you all that he believes about us. He also looks upon you as a traitor to his country."

Fawley was silent for a moment. He appeared to be watching the raindrops upon the window. In reality he was thinking deeply enough. Elida was probably right. It was foolish in these days not to take every precaution with the end of his efforts so closely in sight.

"Whose car is this?" he asked abruptly.

"It belongs to my uncle, the Marchese di Vasena."

"And your destination?"

"The Italian Embassy."

"Sanctuary or prison?" he enquired, with a grim little quiver at the corners of his lips.

"I have thrown in my hand," she told him. "I am no longer to be considered. It is sanctuary only which I offer you."

"But the trouble is," he explained, "that I must go to my rooms. I am leaving England early to-morrow morning, and to say nothing of my kit there are one or two necessary papers—my passport, for instance—which I must take with me."

"I will fetch them for you," she announced. "You yourself—you shall not go. Please be reasonable."

She leaned towards him. Some little quiver in her tone, perhaps the eager flash of her eyes, the closeness of her obscure presence, reminded Fawley that after all he was quite a human person. He took her hand and held it in his.

"My dear Elida," he said, "we have been on opposite sides all this time. How can I let you play around with my papers and learn my secrets?"

"There are no secrets to be learnt from any papers you leave around," she declared. "Besides, you need not mind my seeing anything. I told you just now I have finished with the game. I have an idea in my mind that you are playing for greater stakes than any of us, that we must all seem like little pawns on the chessboard to you. I am content. I will help you if I can, and, to begin with, let me convince you of this—Pietro is absolutely and seriously insane."

"Of course that might complicate matters," Fawley reflected. "As just an angry man I had no fear of him. You see, here in London a man cannot commit murder and get away with it. He cannot even manage an abduction. Patoni in his sane moments would realise that. If he is really mad, however, that is a different matter. The cleverest schemes in the world have been most often foiled by madmen."

"What you will do is this," she said decidedly. "You will come with me to my uncle's. I shall establish you in my rooms. There is no reason to bring the Embassy into the matter at all. You will then telephone your servant what things you require, and if there is anything he is unable to do, you can send me. What time do you start in the morning?"

"Now you see, I prove that I am the worst Secret Service agent in the world because I tell you the whole truth. I am leaving from Heston to-morrow morning at six o'clock."

"Excellent," she replied. "I shall not believe that you are an enemy and I shall not treat you as one. You shall have your short sleep at the Embassy, this car will take you to Heston in the morning, then you must find your adventure, whatever it may be. While you are in danger, I shall be unhappy. When it is all over, I hope that you will come back. I hope," she added, with her fingers upon his shoulders drawing him towards her, "that you will come back to me."

The car drew up smoothly outside the pillared portico of Chester House. A footman came out and opened the door. Fawley followed his guide up the broad steps and into the hall.

CHAPTER XXVI

FAWLEY found his reception by the Minister who in those days was controlling the destinies of France chilling in the extreme. Monsieur Fleuriot, a man of some presence but with a tired expression and an ominous sagging of flesh under his eyes, rose from his chair as Fawley was ushered in, but made no attempt to shake hands. He indicated a chair in cursory fashion.

"It is very good of you to receive me, sir," Fawley remarked.

"I do so," was the cold reply, "with the utmost reluctance. I can refuse no request from the representative of a friendly nation, especially as Monsieur Willoughby Johns is a personal friend of mine, and I believe a friend of France. I must confess, however, that it would have appeared to me a more fitting thing to have found you a prisoner in a French fortress than to be receiving you here."

Fawley smiled deprecatingly.

"I can quite understand your sentiments, sir," he said. "I am only hoping that my explanation may alter your views."

"My views as to spies, especially partially successful ones who are working against my country, are unchangeable."

"But I hope to convince you, sir," Fawley argued earnestly, "that even during the enterprise of which you have, of course, been made acquainted, I was never an enemy of France. I am not an enemy of any nation. If any man could—to borrow the modern shibboleth—call himself an internationalist, it is I."

"To avoid a confusion of ideas, sir," Monsieur Fleuriot said, "I beg that you will proceed with the business which has procured for you this extraordinary letter of introduction. It is the first time, I should think, in history that the leader of a great nation has been asked to receive anyone in your position."

"The world has reached a point," Fawley remarked, "when the old conditions must fall away. Have I your permission to speak plainly?"

"By all means."

"Amongst the great nations of the world," Fawley continued, "France is to-day the most important military power. I do not believe that it is in any way a natural instinct of the French people to crave for bloodshed and disruption and all the horrible things that follow in the wake of war. I believe it is because you have a deep and unchangeable conviction that your country stands in peril."

"You may be right," Monsieur Fleuriot observed dryly. "And then?"

"France, if peace were assured," Fawley went on, "would take the same place amongst the nations of the world in culture and power as she possesses now in military supremacy. She would be a happier and a freer country without this burden of apprehension."

"France fears nobody."

"For a dictum that is excellent," Fawley replied, "but in its greatest significance I deny it. France must fear the re-opening of the bloody days of '14. She must fear the loss again of millions of her subjects. I want you to believe this if you can, Monsieur Fleuriot. I have been working as a secret service agent for the last five years and I have worked with no country's interests at heart. I have worked solely and simply for peace."

"You imagine," Monsieur Fleuriot demanded incredulously, "that you are working in the cause of peace when you steal into the defences of our frontiers and discover our military secrets?"

"I do indeed," Fawley asserted earnestly. "If you think that I behaved like a traitor to France, what then about Italy? But for my efforts I firmly believe, and I can bring forward a great deal of evidence in support of what I say, that a treaty would have been signed before now between Italy and Germany, and it would have been signed by the chief of the monarchist party in Germany, and on the day after its signature she would have pledged herself to the restoration of the Hohenzollern régime. That treaty now will, I hope, never be signed. Behrling will not sign it if he knows the truth, which I can tell him. Italy will not offer to share in it if you will adopt my views and do as I beg. Now, if I may, I am going to speak more bluntly."

"Proceed," Fleuriot begged.

"France believes herself practically secure," Fawley continued. "Her spies have been well informed. She knew a year ago that Italy was collecting aeroplanes, not only of her own manufacture, but from every nation in the world who had skill enough to build them. Even the Soviet Government of Russia contributed, I believe, something like two hundred."

Fawley paused, but his listener gave no sign. The former continued:

"France knew very well the Italian scheme—to launch an attack of a thousand aeroplanes which would pass the frontier with ease and which would lay Nice, Toulon and Marseilles in ruins and the greater portion of the French fleet at the bottom of the sea. Meanwhile, the Italian land forces would have joined the German and attacked across the western frontier. I will not say that France has waited for the day with equanimity, but at any rate she has awaited it without despair. I know the reason why, Monsieur Fleuriot, and it is a secret which should have cost me my life a dozen times over. As it is, the fact that my espionage on your frontier was successful may save the world. You see, I know why you are calm. You have there as well as the guns, as well as all the ordinary defences, you have there an example of the greatest scientific invention which the world of destruction has ever known. You know very well that the hellnotter on the Sospel slopes could destroy by itself, without the help of a single gun, every one of those thousand aeroplanes, whether they passed in the clouds directly overhead or a hundred miles out at sea."

Monsieur Fleuriot had half risen to his feet. He sat down again, breathing quickly. There were little beads of perspiration upon his forehead.

"Mon Dieu!" he muttered.

He dabbed his face with a highly perfumed handkerchief. Fawley paused for a moment.

"I am now going to propose to you, Monsieur Fleuriot," he said, "the most unusual, the most striking gesture which has ever been made in the history of warfare. I am going to suggest to you that you put France in the place of honour amongst the nations of the world as the country who ensured peace. You may sit quiet, you may destroy this scheme at the cost of thousands of lives, you may send a thrill of horror throughout the world, but you can do something more. You can invite representatives of the Italian army to witness the demonstration of what your diabolical machine will do in friendly fashion upon your frontier. If you will do that, there will be no war. Italy would never face the destruction of her aeroplanes. She will abandon her enterprise and the treaty between Behrling and Italy will never be signed."

"It seems to me that you are raving, Major Fawley," the Minister declared.

"What I am saying is the simplest of common sense, Monsieur Fleuriot," Fawley answered. "I will tell you why.

You have been deceived by your great professor. You believe that you possess the only constructed hellnotter in the world. You are wrong. Germany has one completed at Essen. I have seen it with my own eyes."

"It is incredible," Fleuriot exclaimed.

"It is the truth," was the impressive assurance. "And I will tell you this. Von Salzenburg has kept from Italy the secret of their possession. That I shall be able to prove to Berati and his master if you fall in with my scheme. Germany, if her alliance with Italy were an honourable one, would have disclosed the fact of her possession of this duplicate machine. She is too jealous, or rather Von Salzenburg was too jealous for them. It was so mighty a secret that they declined to share it with an ally. Mind you, I will not say that Von Salzenburg knew that you too possessed this horrible machine; but, wilfully or not wilfully, he was keeping a secret from his ally which would have given her the greatest shock of her history."

"Put your proposition into plain words," Monsieur Fleuriot requested.

"I propose that you give me letters to your Colonel Dumesnil commanding the frontier, which will instruct him to make the experiment I suggest, and I further suggest that you address an invitation to the Italian War Office to witness the experiment. Show them what you can do and I guarantee the rest. There will be no war now nor at any time during the near future."

Fleuriot was silent for at least five minutes. He was leaning back in his chair. He had the appearance of a man exhausted by some stupendous brain effort.

"The military staff," he muttered at last, "would scoff at your scheme. War has to come, and nothing can keep Europe free from it. Of that we are all convinced. Why not let it come now? There might be worse moments."

"Monsieur Fleuriot," Fawley said earnestly, "I come now to more concrete things. I come to information of great value, not to information which I gained through espionage, but from the mouth of your friend the British Prime Minister, from the mouth of the Ambassador of my own country in London. The one sane and possible scheme for the preservation of peace is already launched. When Italy knows that her aeroplanes are doomed to destruction, that the ally with whom she was about to conclude a treaty is keeping secret information from her, she will follow in the wake of the others. She will elect for peace. When Germany realises this and many other things, she too will give in. There will be a world pact for peace, and the guarantors will be America, England, France, Germany and Italy. Each of these countries will elect a dictator or a president or, in the case of the royalist countries, the King to sign the pact that under no circumstances will they embark upon war in any shape or form. Listen, Monsieur Fleuriot," Fawley went on, as he noticed the blank expression upon the Minister's face. "I am not talking of dreams or fancies. The scheme has been carried beyond that world. The pact is actually drawn up and there are signatures already upon it. The President of the United States has signed. Those responsible for the destinies of Great Britain have done the same thing. That document is now in the safe at the British Foreign Office. It awaits the signatures of yourself and Monsieur Flaubert the President, the signatures of Italy and Germany. Adopt my scheme, Monsieur Fleuriot, and that pact is going to be the mightiest ruling force in the world. Give Italy that demonstration. Let it be brought to her notice that the country with whom she was seeking an alliance has deceived her and she will sign. Behrling hates war. That was the reason why Berati was favouring the monarchist party in Germany. Behrling will sign the pact, so will Hindenburg. Now, Monsieur Fleuriot, will you write to Colonel Dumesnil? Will you place the arrangements for carrying out the experiment in my hands? Remember the secret of the mountains of Sospel is no longer a secret. Even though you shoot me before sundown, as I suppose you have the right to do, you will not save that secret."

The Minister rose from his place. He walked to the window and looked out for a few minutes across the gardens. Then he came back and resumed his seat. With trembling fingers he lit a cigarette. He was a man of courteous habits, but he offered no invitation to his guest.

"Major Fawley," he confided, "for the last half-hour I have not been quite sure whether I have been listening to a madman or not. All that you have told me is possible, of course. It is nevertheless incredible."

Fawley smiled.

"Naturally," he said, "you require some verification of my word. The English Ambassador, Lord Rollins, is waiting to hear from you. He will tell you that he has seen the signatures of which I have already told you. It is a simple document. There will be a secondary one of conditions, but nothing will alter the vital principle. The five powerful nations of the world swear each one that whatever provocation they receive, there shall be no war. It is enough."

"Lord Rollins, you said? The English Ambassador?" Fleuriot exclaimed.

"He is spending the afternoon at home in case you care to send for him."

"You have at least given me an issue," the Minister cried out in relief. "I will receive Lord Rollins at once. There shall be a Cabinet meeting following his visit. If yours has been an honest enterprise, Major Fawley, I consent to your scheme. If I find that you are still playing the game of the super-Secret Service man, you will be shot, as you say, before sundown, and if your Ambassador went down on his knees to save you he would do so in vain."

"Excellent," Fawley agreed. "Place me under arrest if you like. I am content."

Monsieur Fleuriot touched his bell.

"I shall not order your arrest, Major Fawley, but I shall place you in security," he said. "Meanwhile, I shall send for Lord Rollins."

The Minister held whispered conference with his secretary, who had answered the bell. The latter turned to Fawley.

"If Monsieur will be so kind as to come to my room," he begged.

At the door Fawley looked back. Monsieur Fleuriot had still the appearance of a man stunned. In a way, however, there was a change in his features, a light upon his face. If this thing should be true, it would be he who would lead France into the new world!

CHAPTER XXVII

FAWLEY brought his Lancia slowly to a standstill at the top of the Sospel Pass. He was surrounded now by the white-capped mountains of the Lesser Alps and, though the day had been warm enough, the evening breeze brought with it a cold tang from the snows. He paused to light a ciga-rette. The work of mining and tunnelling the mountain range seemed to have progressed even since his last visit. There was a new road cut in the direction of headquar-ters. Within half a mile of him, around the shoulder of the hill, was the subterranean passage from which he had had so narrow an escape. Yet everywhere there seemed to be a curious stillness. There was no sound anywhere of human life or activities. Underneath his feet, almost underneath the whole range of hills around which the road wound, was another world—an active world bristling with the great vehicles of destruction. From where he sat he could see the ravine down which he had flung himself only a month or so ago. He could recall the sound of the rifle bullets spitting against the rocks, the muttering of the Chasseurs Alpins cursing the darkness. He had escaped where others with as much experience as he had paid with their lives for seeking to learn the secrets of this fortress. Would the luck hold, he wondered.

Tramp! Tramp! Tramp! The sound of men marching close at hand. Fawley, suddenly alert, sat up in his place. They were already making their way around the corner, a little company of weary men with a handful of tired mules. They were almost passing him when the officer who was marching in the middle of the road came to a sudden standstill. He looked incredulously at Fawley. It was the same officer who had found him wandering in the roads and taken him to the Colonel! The meeting was one of mutual amazement. The young Lieutenant of the Chasseurs Alpins, however, was this time a very resolute person. He snapped out his orders. In a very few seconds Fawley found himself with a soldier standing on each footboard and another with pointed rifle facing the car.

"What's the trouble?" Fawley asked.

"You are under arrest," the officer replied. "I do not think I could possibly bring in a more welcome prisoner. Start your car, if you please, take the turn to the right and stop at headquarters. You heard my orders to the men. They will shoot unless you obey precisely."

Fawley made no comment. He started the engine and drove slowly along in the direction indicated. When he arrived at the white-plastered house from which was flying the French flag, he descended and was escorted, the centre of a strong bodyguard, into the bare apartment which he had visited once before. The same Commandant was seated at his table with a similar pile of despatches before him and an orderly on either side. This time, however, Fawley's reception was different. The Colonel stared at him first in blank astonishment, then a curious glitter of almost malicious gratification flashed in his eyes.

"*Le bon Dieu!*" he exclaimed. "It is the same man!"

Fawley saluted with a smile.

"It is quite true. I was here a month or so ago, Colonel," he reminded him. "Major Fawley, late of the American Army."

The Colonel's fingers caressed his moustache.

"Ah yes," he said. "I remember you. Major Fawley, of the American Army. Excellent! You came, I think, to buy the Sospel Golf-links."

"Exactly," Fawley admitted. "I have almost made up my mind to sacrifice my deposit, however. Your work up here is too threatening. I can see that Sospel might become a strategic point if a rapid advance were contemplated."

The Colonel murmured softly to himself. His eyes travelled past Fawley to the door.

"Close the door," he ordered. "See that it is securely fastened. Search the prisoner for arms."

"Arms," Fawley protested. "Why should I carry arms?"

"The man is a *blagueur*," the Colonel said harshly. "Search him for arms and papers."

Fawley felt himself pinioned from behind. He yielded without any attempt at resistance. A cigarette-case, a small revolver and a long official-looking envelope were produced and laid upon the table.

"A revolver," Fawley argued, "is almost a necessity in this country. I motor a great deal at night. I have never used it, but one must threaten if a bandit accosts one."

The Colonel pushed the weapon impatiently on one side, took up the envelope, and if his astonishment at seeing Fawley was great his astonishment as he studied the envelope was certainly greater. He turned it over in his hand time after time. It bore the well-known official seal of the Quai d'Orsay and it was addressed to himself!

> "*Colonel Dumesnil*
> *By favour of Major Martin Fawley.*"

"A communication for you," Fawley explained courteously. "I was on my way to deliver it."

"Perhaps!" the Colonel exclaimed contemptuously. "It is a likely story that! This is one more of your artifices, I make no doubt. Lieutenant Vigny, detail a squad of men in the courtyard with loaded rifles. We do not let a spy slip through our hands twice, Major Fawley."

"I think," the latter suggested, "you had better open that envelope."

"I shall do so," the Colonel assured him, "but this time you have been too clever. I shall take nothing for granted. Before I read I shall be convinced that what I read is forgery."

"Forgeries in a code so secret as the French 'B' military code do not exist," Fawley declared. "I received that envelope from Marshal Hugot himself three days ago."

"How do you know that it is in the French military code?" the Colonel demanded.

"The Minister for War, Field-marshal Hugot, himself told me so," Fawley explained. "There was no need for me to open the letter. I know exactly what it contains."

"You have dared to present yourself at the Quai d'Orsay?" the Colonel gasped.

"I had a very pleasant hour there on Monday," was the prompt reply.

"If I have my will," the Colonel said, as he broke the seal, "you will have a far less pleasant few minutes shortly looking down the barrels of my men's rifles! You may fool a French soldier once, Major Fawley. It is not an easy thing to do the second time."

The Colonel slit open the long envelope and drew out a closely written sheet of paper. He frowned as he stared at it. Without a doubt it was a communication addressed in the most secret of all codes, a code known only to the inner circle of the French military council.

"Fetch me Manual 17 from the safe," he directed one of the orderlies.

The man obeyed. The Colonel opened the volume and, producing a fresh sheet of paper, carefully commenced his task of transcribing. His occupation lasted for something like twenty minutes. When he had finished, he read through the decoded letter word for word, tapping each with his pencil. He had the appearance of a man suffering from shock.

"It is impossible," he muttered to himself. The palm of one hand rested on the decoded message, the palm of the other on the message itself. He leaned forward in his chair. His eyes seemed to be boring into Fawley's.

"When did you receive this communication?" he demanded.

"Monday at eight o'clock from the hands of Field marshal Hugot himself."

"It is impossible," the Colonel declared. "Marshal Hugot is at Geneva."

"He may be now," Fawley answered indifferently. "He flew back from Geneva to Paris on Sunday. I had an interview with him at mid-night. He placed this communication in my hands to be brought to you."

"You know what is written here?"

"Absolutely," Fawley assured him. "The suggestion itself came from me. I will admit," he went on thoughtfully, "that my reception at the Quai d'Orsay, in the first instance, was not everything I could have wished. That perhaps is natural. There were certain things against me, including your own very bitter report of my innocent activities, Colonel. But, you see, I had credentials. I was able to impress them upon the Staff."

The Colonel breathed heavily several times. Then he looked up again.

"I decline," he decided, "even in the face of such evidence, to accept this as genuine."

"Then you are a very obstinate person," Fawley replied. "You have plenty of ways of securing verification, but I suggest that you use the speediest. The matter referred to in that communication is one that brooks of no delay."

The Colonel turned towards his senior orderly.

"Pierre," he directed, "call up the Department on our private long-distance wire. Say that I must speak to General du Vivier himself."

The man saluted and hurried out. The Colonel leaned back in his chair.

"Your story will be put to the proof," he said coldly.

"A reasonable precaution," Fawley murmured. "May I, however, be allowed to sit down and, more especially, to smoke?"

The Colonel bit his lips.

"You may sit down in that chair facing the barred window," he enjoined, "and you may watch those twelve men standing at attention. You know what their orders will be in the event of there being the slightest hitch in these communications. Orderly, take these cigarettes to the prisoner."

"Prisoner," Fawley repeated reproachfully, as he accepted the case and lit a cigarette. "Well, prisoner if you like," he added. "Liberty will be all the more desirable."

"It is my personal wish," the Colonel acknowledged, "that that liberty never comes. I am not a cruel man, but I should stand at the window there and watch your execution with the utmost satisfaction. If this letter is genuine, it will simply prove to me that you are something of a necromancer in your line. I shall still believe that you have deceived my chiefs as you have deceived us."

"You may believe that, Colonel," Fawley said quietly, "but you will be wrong."

There was a long silence. The Colonel continued his task of signing papers and the sound of the scratching of his pen was almost the only sound in the room. The window itself commanded a view of the dusty courtyard, and the sun flashed upon the short-barrelled rifles of the men waiting to perform their task. It was a silent spot, this, amongst the mountains. If engineering works were still being carried on in the vicinity, the labours of the day were evidently at an end. From somewhere in the heart of the woods came the faintly musical humming of a saw at work amongst the pine logs, and from an incredible distance came every now and then the faint wailing of a siren in the midst of a stretch of misty sea. Fawley smoked on composedly. Only once he indulged in a grimace. He remembered the story of a fellow-worker who, after bringing off many successful coups, was eventually shot for being discovered with absolutely genuine papers. Those things are in the day's march. It might come to him as it had come to others. Fawley, in moments of crisis, had contemplated often before the problem of sudden extermination. This time it was mixed with a new emotion. He found himself remembering Elida!

An orderly hurried in. He whispered a word in the Colonel's ear. The latter left his place and entered the little cabinet at the far end of the room. He remained inside fully ten minutes. One heard occasionally the threads of a broken conversation mingled with the somewhat heated amenities between the Colonel and the local authorities. In the end the Colonel emerged from the telephone booth and resumed his seat behind his desk without speech. He had the air of a man who has received a sudden and unexpected blow. He had lost his dignity, his poise, his military flair. He was just a middle-aged, tired old gentleman who had set himself to face an unsatisfactory problem.

"Do I take off my collar," Fawley asked, "and submit myself to the amiable ministrations of your picturesque bandits outside, or are you by chance convinced that my mission to you is a genuine one?"

The Colonel closed his eyes for a moment as though in pain.

"I am prepared to admit the genuineness of your mission, Major Fawley," he said. "Why my superiors at the War Office are playing this extraordinary game I do not know. I imagine that military logic has become subservient to political intrigue.... What date do you propose for this extraordinary entertainment?"

"Sunday next. Four days from to-day," Fawley answered briskly. "Of course, before that time I have an almost impossible task to perform, but if I should succeed—four days from to-day. You will do me the favour perhaps to look at this small sketch. You will see I have marked in pencil three crosses just where I should think I might install our friends the enemy."

The Colonel studied the plan. He referred to a hand-drawn map and turned back again to the plan. He nodded his head slowly in unconvinced but portentous fashion.

"With every moment of our intercourse," he said coldly, "you impress me the more, Major Fawley, with your exceptional ability as a—do we call it spy or secret-service star? I leave it to you to choose. Be there at that spot at the time and hour appointed and France, with your assistance, shall betray herself."

Fawley rose to his feet.

"I gather that I am a free man?" he asked.

"You are a free man," the Colonel answered calmly. "I do not like you. I do not trust you. I hate these intermeshed political and military eruptions which in a single second destroy the work of years. In letting you go free I submit to authority, but if you care for a warning, take it. You are a self-acknowledged spy. You will be watched from the moment you leave my doors, and if the time should come when you make that little slip which they say all men of your profession make sooner or later, I pray that I may be the one to benefit."

Fawley sighed as he drew himself up and stood with his hand upon the door-handle.

"I really do not know, Colonel," he expostulated, "why you dislike me so much. I need not have worked at all. I have chosen to work in the greatest cause the world has ever known—the great cause of peace. I have already risked my life a half-dozen times. Once more makes no difference. Perhaps when you have settled down on your estates with your children and grandchildren you will not regard the man who works behind the scenes quite so venomously.... By the by, if I must submit to perpetual escort, may I beg that you will give me two of your lightest guards? The two who mounted my footboard coming up would break the back axle of my car before we reached Sospel."

The Colonel looked coldly at his departing guest.

"You need have no fear, Major Fawley," he said. "You are no longer a prisoner. My motor-bicycle scouts will trace you from the moment you leave to wherever you go and telephone to me their report. I shall get in touch at once with the Chef de la Sûreté of the district. Things may happen or they may not."

Fawley drew a deep breath of the pine-scented air as he stood outside, lingered for a moment and stepped unhindered into his car. This was the first stage of his desperate mission safely accomplished. Elida had warned him almost passionately that it was the second which would prove most difficult.

CHAPTER XXVIII

ONCE more Fawley crossed that huge, spacious apartment at the far end of which Berati sat enthroned behind his low desk, a grim and motionless figure. The chair on his left-hand side was vacant. There was no sign anywhere of Patoni.

"I ought to apologise for my sudden return to Rome, perhaps," Fawley ventured. "Events marched quicker than I had anticipated. Except for a brief stay at Monte Carlo, I have come here directly from Paris."

Berati leaned slightly forward. His eyes were like slits of coal-black fire, his lower lip was dragged down, his face resembled a sculptor's effort to reproduce the human sneer.

"You have been paying quite a round of visits, I understand," he remarked icily. "London—I scarcely thought that London and Downing Street were places with which we had any present concern."

"You were misinformed, sir," Fawley replied calmly. "London and Washington are both concerned in the present situation."

Berati rang a bell from under his desk, an unseen gesture. In complete silence, so stealthily that Fawley was unaware of their presence until he felt a heavy hand upon each of his shoulders, two of the new Civic Guards had entered the room and moved up to where he stood. They were standing on either side of him now—portents of the grim future.

"You and the Princess," Berati said harshly, "both of you pretend to have been working for Italy. You have been working for England. The Princess, for all I know, has been working for France——"

"Not exactly correct, sir," Fawley interrupted. "Of the Princess's activities I know little except that I believe she was trying to coerce you into signing a treaty with the wrong party in Germany. So far as I am concerned, I will admit that I have deceived you. I professed to enter your service. I never had the intention of working for one nation only. I had what I venture to consider a greater cause at heart."

Berati glared at him from behind his desk. He seemed to have suddenly become, in these moments of unrestrained anger, the living presentment of the caricatures of himself which Europe had studied with shivering repugnance for the last two years.

"There is one thing about you, Major Fawley," he said. "There will not be many words between us, so I will pay you a compliment. I think that you are the bravest man I ever met."

"You flatter me," Fawley murmured.

"Somehow or other," Berati went on, "you learnt the most important secrets of the French fortifications. You must have taken enormous risks. I sent five men after you to check your statements, and every one of them lies buried amongst the mountains. Yours was a wonderful and courageous effort, but your visit here to-day is perhaps a braver action still. Do you realise that, Fawley? You must have known that if ever you came within my reach—within my grasp—you would pay for your treachery with your life."

"I knew there was a risk," Fawley admitted coolly. "On the other hand, I know that you have brains. I am less afraid of you than I should be of most men, because I think that when you have listened to what I have to say you will probably widen your view. You will realise that the person whom you accuse of betraying her has saved Italy."

"Fine talk," Berati sneered.

"Never in my life," Fawley assured him, "have I made a statement which I could not prove. What I am going to disclose now is the greatest secret which has existed in Europe for a hundred years. If it is your wish that I should continue in the presence of these men, I will do so. For reasons of policy I should advise you to send them away. I am unarmed: your person is sacred from me. I give you my word as an American officer that I shall not raise my hand to save my life. I do pray for one thing, however, and that is that the few words I have to say now are spoken for your ear only."

"Search this man for arms," Berati commanded.

Fawley held out his hands. The two guards went over him carefully. The contents of his pockets were laid out upon the table.

"The Signor has no weapon," one of the two men announced.

"Wait outside the door," Berati ordered.

The men retired. Fawley returned the various articles they had left upon the table to his pockets. He waited until the door was closed.

"General Berati," he said, "on the twenty-fourth of May or thereabouts you intended to launch the most amazing aeroplane attack which history has ever dreamed of—some thousand aeroplanes were to have destroyed utterly Nice, Toulon and Marseilles and swept round upon Paris. A German army, munitioned and armed by Soviet Russia, was to have joined hands with forty divisions of Italians upon the eastern frontier of France. Roughly these were your plans."

"It is fortunate indeed," Berati sneered, "that the man who knows them so well is the man who is about to die."

"We are all about to die," was the indifferent response. "The length of our lives is merely a figure of speech. In comparison with the cause for which I am fighting, my life is as valueless as a handful of dust."

There was a light in Fawley's eyes which Berati had never seen before. In spite of himself he was impressed.

"What is this cause of yours?" he asked.

"By this time you should have known," Fawley answered. "Remember, I went through the war. I started as an ardent soldier. The profession of arms was to me almost a sacred one. I took it as an axiom that the waging of war alone could decide the destinies of the world. I came out at the end of the war a broken man. The horror of it had poisoned my blood. For two years I was recovering my health mentally and physically. I came back into the world a crank if you like, a missionary if you will, but at any rate a man with a single desperate purpose. It made a man of me once again. My own life became, as I have told you, worthless except in so far as I could use it to carry out my purposes. Washington alone knew the truth, and they thought me crazy. Two people in England divined it. To the official classes of every other nation in Europe I was just a Secret Service agent working for himself, for his own advancement, and because he loved the work. Italy—I came to you. I cared nothing for Italy. Germany—I went to Germany. I cared nothing for Germany. France—I very nearly mortally offended, but I cared nothing for France. What I did care for was to cherish the great ambition which has come to fruition after years of suffering. To do something—to devote every atom of energy remaining to me in life—to tear out of the minds of men this poisonous idea that war is the sane and inevitable method of dealing with international disputes."

Berati sat with his chin raised upon his hand, sprawling across the table, his eyes fixed upon his visitor.

"France has made the first sacrifice," the latter went on. "I am hoping that Italy will make the second. I ask you to send a messenger, General Berati, across to the French Embassy and to request them to hand you a letter which they are holding, addressed to you in my care. I tell you frankly that I dared not bring it myself across the frontier or travel with it to Rome, but the letter is there. When you see what it contains, I will finish my explanation."

"That means," Berati said, "that I shall have to keep you alive for another half an hour?"

"It would be advisable," Fawley acquiesced.

CHAPTER XXIX

DOWN on the coast the marvellous chain of lights along the Promenade des Anglais and the illumination of Monte Carlo shone pale in the steady moonlight, but up in the clefts of the mountains by the straggling frontier line the mists were rolling and at the best there were occasional glimpses of a vaporous twilight. From down in the deep valleys came the booming of a dying mistral. Stars were few—only the reflection of a shrouded moon wrapped at times in a sort of ghostly illumination the white-topped caps of the distant mountains. Berati shivered in his fur coat as he leaned back in the open touring car. Fawley, pacing the road, continually glanced skywards. The two other men—one a staff officer of the Italian Flying command, the other a field-marshal of the army—scarcely took their eyes from the clouds. In the distance was a small escort of Chasseurs Alpins. They stood like dumb figures at the bend of the curving road, veritable gnomes of the darkness in their military cloaks and strange uniform. There was no need for silence, but no one spoke. It was Berati at last who broke through the tension.

"It is the hour?" he asked.

"Within five minutes," Fawley answered.

"We run some risk here, perhaps?" Berati continued in his thin, querulous voice.

"An experiment like this must always entail risk of some sort," the staff officer observed.

Dumesnil held a small electric torch to his watch.

"The first should be here in ten minutes," he announced.

"Guido Pellini is the pilot," Berati muttered.

"Much too brave a man to be the victim of such a ghastly enterprise," one of the Italian staff officers declared.

"I agree with you," Fawley said emphatically. "It was Air-Marshal Bastani here who insisted upon the test being carried out in such a fashion. It was he who asked for the ten volunteers."

"I asked only," the Marshal announced harshly, "for what our brave Italian soldiers offer always freely—the risk of their lives for the good of their country. I myself have a nephew in the clouds somewhere."

Someone whispered a warning. There was an intense silence. They all heard what sounded like the muffled thunder of a coming earthquake from the sides of the mountain. The ground beneath their feet trembled, startled birds flew over their heads. From the unseen distance they heard, too, the trampling of a flock of goats or sheep galloping madly towards the valley. The sound died away.

"The dynamos," Fawley muttered. "The hellnotter is at work."

They listened again. Another sound became audible, a sound at first like the ticking of a watch, then unmistakable.

Somewhere in the hidden world above an aeroplane was travelling. Everyone was now standing in the road. Berati was breathing heavily. The excitement amongst the group was such that Bastani, the Chief of the Italian Air Staff, found himself moaning with pent-up anxiety. Then, when their eyes were red with the strain of watching, there shot into the sky a long, ever-widening shaft of light—pale violet light—which seemed to illuminate nothing but stayed like a ghastly finger piercing the clouds. There was a second rush of light, this time towards the sea. The intervening clouds seemed to melt away with its passage until it burst like a rocket into a mass of incongruous flame and then passed onwards and upwards. Through the silence of the night came a crash from the other side of the precipice as though a meteor had fallen. The staff officer saluted.

"A brave man," he muttered, "dead!"

"It was a ghastly test, this," Fawley observed sorrowfully. "There was no need. The thing could have been proved without human sacrifice."

Again there came the sound of that horrible, nerve-shattering crash. This time closer at hand. They even fancied that they heard a human cry. Fawley would have stepped into his car, but the staff officer by his side checked him.

"They were flying at over two thousand feet," he said. "No one could live till the end."

Fawley pointed upwards to where that faint violet light seemed to have discoloured the whole sky.

"You see that area, General," he pointed out. "Nothing living could exist within it. No form of explosive could be there which would not ignite. No metal that would not be disintegrated. The man who works the hellnotter has no need to aim. He has an illimitable range, a range which in theory might reach the stars and a field of ever-increasing miles as the ray flashes. A hellnotter is the last word in horrors. It has been your own choice to sacrifice your men, but you will not find a single machine which exists except in charred fragments, or a single recognisable human being. If the squadron to-night, instead of ten aeroplanes, had consisted of a thousand, the result would have been precisely the same. There would not have been a human being alive or a wing of a machine to tell the story."

Fawley spoke with no elation—sorrowfully though convincingly. Berati spoke only once, and his thoughts seemed far away.

"Von Salzenburg knew. God!"

The violet tinge in the sky seemed to lean in their direction. There was a warning shout from Fawley. In a crowd they dashed into the wide opening of the shelter outside which the cars had stopped. Fawley called out to them.

"Keep well away from the mouth," he directed. "There was one about a mile up. I heard the humming."

His voice echoed and re-echoed down the smoothly tunnelled aperture. Bastani opened his lips to reply, but for the next few moments no speech was possible. From outside came a sound like the battering of the earth by some gigantic flail, the crashing of metal striking the rocks, the roar of an explosion. An unnatural calm fell upon them all. They were in almost complete darkness, but when Berati pulled out his electric torch their faces were like white masks in the velvety blackness. Outside in a matter of seconds the fierce rain had ceased. There was the hissing and crackling of flames, a lurid light which for the moment showed them the whole countryside. The silence, which lasted for a few seconds, was broken once more by the screaming of birds and the galloping backwards and forwards of terrified cattle. Bastani pushed his way to the front.

"It is my duty to see something of this in the moment of its opening."

The French officer in charge remonstrated violently.

"Marshal Bastani," he begged, "you have been placed in my care. This is all new to us. There may be another explosion. In any case, nothing will have changed if we wait."

Bastani pushed him gently but with force on one side.

"It is my duty," he repeated. "I must be the first to investigate. It is for that that I am here."

He disappeared into the mists outside and they saw the flash of his torch as he turned towards the ascent. The French officer shrugged his shoulders.

"You will bear witness, gentlemen, that I did my best to stop the Marshal. We have had no experience in the after-events of such a cataclysm as this."

They talked in desultory fashion. Berati smoked furiously. The seconds were drawn out. Conversation was spasmodic and disconnected. Then Fawley, who was nearest to the entrance, pointed out a thin pencil of light between two mountains eastward.

"The morning comes quickly here," he said. "In half an hour at the most we can leave."

Almost as he spoke there was another explosion, which shook large fragments of rock from the sides of their shelter. In one place the cement floor beneath their feet cracked. Then there was silence.

"I wish Bastani had stayed with us," Berati murmured.

The dawn through which they started their short ride to Colonel Dumesnil's headquarters brought its own peculiar horrors. With every yard they found strange distorted fragments of metal—nothing recognisable. A bar of steel transposed into the likeness of a catherine-wheel. What might have been the wing of an aeroplane rolled up like a sheet of paper. At different points on the mountain-side there were small fires burning. At the last bend they came suddenly upon a man walking round in circles in the road. He wore the rags of a portion of torn uniform. One side of his face was unrecognisable. Blood was dripping from a helpless arm.

"Count Bastani! My God!" one of the Italian staff officers cried.

They were near enough to see him now. He looked at them with wild eyes, threw up one arm and called out. Then, as though he had tripped, he fell backwards heavily. There was plenty of help at hand, but Air-Marshal Bastani was dead.

In the orderly-room of the French headquarters hidden amongst the hills Colonel Dumesnil's secretary was seated typing. Dumesnil himself, who had raced on from the pass, rose to his feet mechanically at their entrance. He handed a sheet of paper to Berati, who was the first to stagger in. The latter waved it away.

"Read it to me," he begged. "My eyes are blind with the horrors they have looked upon."

"It is my first report to headquarters," Dumesnil confided.

> "*I have to report that ten apparently enemy aeroplanes endeavoured to cross the frontier to-night at varying distances. All ten machines were at once destroyed and all pilots are believed to have perished. I regret also to announce that Air-Marshal Luigi Bastani, one of the observers selected by the Italian War Office, having left the shelter provided, was killed by the falling fragments of one of the planes.*
>
> "DUMESNIL,
> "*Colonel.*"

"The Air-Marshal's body was brought in a few minutes ago," the Colonel announced.... "My orderly has prepared coffee in the messroom."

A soldier servant threw open the door of the next room. Somehow or other everyone staggered in that direction. The windows looked across the precipice to the mountains eastward. As they sank into their places the first rays of the rising sun in ribald beauty moved across the snows.

CHAPTER XXX

FAWLEY reached Berlin a tired man with the firm determination, however, to sleep for twenty-four hours. At the end of that time he came back into the world, submitted himself to the full ministrations of an adequate coiffeur, and sent round a note asking for an interview with Heinrich Behrling. There seemed to be some slight hesitation about granting his request, but in the end it was acceded to. Behrling, now established in a palace, received him a little coolly.

"You lacked confidence in me, I fear, Major Fawley," Behrling remarked, motioning him towards a chair but making no effort to shake hands. "Well, you see what has happened. I suppose you know? Some of the newspapers have done their best to hide their heads in the sand, but the truth is all the time there."

"I never lacked confidence in you," Fawley said. "I never doubted your star. You have triumphed as you deserve to triumph. I have come here to make sure that you retain all that you have won."

Behrling moved uneasily in his chair.

"What do you mean—retain what I have won?" he demanded harshly. "There is no question about that."

"Perhaps not," Fawley replied. "At the same time it is necessary that you should forget the satisfaction of small triumphs.

You must rise above them. Italy, if she turned towards anyone, would turn towards you. Any idea of a treaty signed by anyone else on behalf of Germany has been washed out. On the other hand, the treaty itself has vanished."

Behrling looked keenly at his visitor. During the last few weeks the former's appearance had changed. He was wearing well-tailored clothes, his untidy moustache was close cropped, his hair was no longer an unkempt mass; it conformed in its smooth backward brushing to the fashion of the times. Success had agreed with him and he seemed to have gained in dignity and confidence.

"The treaty has been washed out," he repeated meditatively.

"The War Office of Italy has abandoned its scheme," Fawley confided. "I dare say you know that already. If they had made their alliance with Krust and the monarchists, as at one time seemed probable, they would have remained a vassal state for another thirty years. A merciful Providence—I ask your forgiveness for a somewhat slang phrase—put them on a winner. They distrusted Von Salzenburg, and Krust and Berati were never on good terms."

"There was some other happening, though?" Behrling asked, his voice hardening.

"There was never any intention of keeping you in the dark," Fawley assured him, "but naturally they did not want the Press to get hold of it. France issued a private challenge to Italy and Italy accepted it. What happened will always remain a chapter of secret history, but it was a very wonderful chapter. France and Italy have shaken hands. There will be no war."

"Between France and Italy?"

"There will be no war at all."

Behrling sat motionless in his chair. The lines of thought were deeply engraved on his face. He drummed with his fist upon the table. His eyes never left his visitor's. They seemed as though they were trying to bore their way into the back of his mind.

"Germany has yet to speak," he reminded Fawley at last.

"There is no one who knows better than you yourself," the latter said calmly, "that Germany cannot go to war without the alliance of another nation."

"A million of the finest young men any race has ever produced——"

Fawley, who was rarely impetuous in conversation, interrupted almost savagely.

"The most reckless military fanatic who ever breathed, Herr Behrling, would never dare to sacrifice the whole youth of his country in an unequal struggle to gain—God knows what. You are without munitions, a sufficiency of guns, you have not even rifles, you have not the food to support an army, you have not an established commissariat, you have no navy to follow your movements at sea. You cannot make war, Herr Behrling."

Behrling's face was dark with passion.

"Who are you who come here to tell me what I can and cannot do?" he demanded furiously. "You appear first as an envoy of Italy. You are an American who bargains in Downing Street. You were at the Quai d'Orsay a week ago. Whose agent are you? For whom do you work?"

"The time has come for me to answer that question," Fawley replied. "I am glad that you have asked it. I work for no nation. I work for what people have called a dream but which is soon to become reality. I work for the peace of civilised countries and for the peace of Europe."

"You take your instructions from someone," Behrling insisted.

"From no one. Nor do I give instructions. I am here, though, to tell you why there will be no war, if you care to listen."

"There have been rumours of a pact," Behrling remarked cynically. "Pacts I am sick of. They start with acclamation. When the terms are announced, enthusiasm dwindles. In a month or two they are just a pile of parchment."

"The pact I am speaking of has survived all these troubles."

Behrling squared his shoulders.

"Well, tell me about it," he invited with resignation. "I warn you I am no sympathetic listener. I am sick of promises and treaties. The bayonet is the only real olive-branch."

"You will have to forget those crisp little journalistic epigrams if you stay where you are, Behrling," his visitor said firmly.

Behrling was furious. He rose to his feet and pointed towards the door. Fawley shook his head.

"Too late, my friend," he declared. "The pact I am offering you is one already signed at Washington, at Windsor and Downing Street. It has been signed by the President of France and the Premier. It has been signed by the King of Italy and Berati's master. It only remains to have your signature and Hindenburg's."

"Signed?" Behrling repeated incredulously.

"Absolutely. It is the simplest of all pacts that has ever been recorded. The secondary tabulated formula of minor conditions will be issued shortly, but they will none of them affect the main point. America, England, France and Italy have entered into a compact that under no circumstances will they go to war. It is to be a five-Power pact. You are the man for whose signature we are waiting now and the thing is finished."

"Under no circumstances are we to go to war!" Behrling muttered in dazed fashion.

"Well, you see you cannot go to war," Fawley pointed out with a smile, "if there is no one to go to war with."

Behrling waved his hand towards the east window with a sweeping gesture and his companion nodded understandingly.

"Quite so," he admitted. "There is Soviet Russia, but Soviet Russia came into the world spouting peace. With

America and the four civilised nations of Europe united she will scarcely blacken the pages of history by attempting a bellicose attitude. If she did, there is a special clause which would mean for her economic destruction."

Behrling rose from his place and walked restlessly up and down the room. His pride was hurt, his dreams of the future dimmed. The promises he had made his people were to become, then, impossible. He swung round and faced Fawley.

"Look here," he said. "This pact of yours. Well enough for England to sign it—she has all that she needs. Well enough for France—she bled the world in 1919. Well enough for Italy, who could not even conquer Austria and is laden with spoils. What about us? Stripped of everything. The pact comes to us at an evil moment. Peace is great. Peace is a finer condition than warfare—I grant you that; but peace should come at the right moment. It is the wrong moment for Germany."

"Others beside you," Fawley acknowledged, "have seen the matter from that point of view, Behrling. England and America have both discussed it with sympathy. I bring you a great offer—an offer which you can announce as the result of your own policy—a great triumph to salve the humiliation of the country. In consideration of your signing the pact, England will restore to you your colonies."

Behrling resumed his perambulations of the room. His heart was lighter. This man with the quiet voice and the indescribable sense of power spoke the truth. War was an impossibility. Here was something to send the people crazy with delight, to make them forget the poison of Versailles. Behrling knew as well as any German how, apart from their intrinsic value, the thought of foreign possessions had always thrilled his country-people. The Polish Corridor—nothing. A matter of arrangement. But the colonies back again! The jewels set once more in her crown, and he—Behrling—the man to proclaim this great happening as the result of his own diplomacy. He resumed his seat.

"Major Fawley," he said, "I suppose in all history there has never been a case of an unknown ambassador like you speaking with a voice of such colossal authority. You are known to the world only as an American Secret Service agent who became a free lance and betrayed the country for whom he worked."

"In her own interests," his visitor reminded him, "and in the interests of the world. That is true. But I do not ask you to take my word. It is not I who will bring you the treaty or lead you to it. You will find it at the English Ambassador's or the American Embassy, I am not sure which. Five minutes will tell us. You can sign it to-day. You can lunch with Martin-Green, the American Ambassador, where you will probably meet Lord Inglewood, the Englishman. You can sign it to-day and issue your proclamation to the German people this afternoon. You will have the largest crowd that

Germany has ever known shouting outside your residence tonight. The coming of peace to the world, after all, Behrling, is the greatest boon that could happen. I only deal with superficials. You will meet the councillors at both Embassies during the day. You will understand much that I cannot tell you. But nothing can dim the truth. This is peace. And however you may talk, Behrling," Fawley went on, after a momentary break in his voice, "of the military spirit, the grand sense of patriotism that comes from the souls of the German people, you know and they all know in their calm moments that they too are fathers, they too have their own little circle of friends and shudder at the thought of being robbed of them. War may have its glories. They fade away into blatant vapours if you compare them with the splendours of the peaceful, well-ordered life—the arts progressing, manufactories teeming with work and life, the peoples of every nation blessed without ever-haunting anxiety."

Behrling smiled and there was little of the grimness left in his face.

"You are eloquent, my doyen of Secret Service men," he observed.

Fawley smiled back.

"I think," he said, "that it is the longest speech I ever made in my life."

Behrling was holding the telephone in his hand. He touched a bell and demanded the presence of his secretary.

Already he was on fire, yet even in that moment he seemed scarcely able to take his eyes off his visitor.

"After all," he remarked, with a smile half-whimsical, half-jealous at the corners of his lips, "you will be the outstanding figure in this business."

Fawley shook his head.

"My name will never be heard," he declared. "I shall remain what I have been all my life—the Secret Service agent."

CHAPTER XXXI

THE Marchese Marius di Vasena, Italian Ambassador to the Court of St. James's, threw himself into an easy-chair with a sigh of relief. This was the moment for which he had been waiting more or less patiently since the night when he had sheltered Martin Fawley, and Fawley in return had taken him a little way into his confidence, had raised for him with careful and stealthy fingers the curtain which shrouded a Utopian future.... From outside the folding doors came the sound of floods of music distant and near at hand, the shuffling of feet, the subdued hum of happy voices, the fluttering of women's dresses like the winged passage of a flock of doves.

"We make history, my friends," the Marchese exclaimed, with a gesture which would have been dramatic if he himself, like most of the diplomats and politicians of the five countries, had not been somewhat overtired.

"What sort of a chapter in the world's history, I wonder," Prince von Fürstenheim, German Ambassador, speculated. "I have been present at many functions organised to celebrate the launching of a new war. I have never yet heard of a great entertainment like this given to celebrate the coming of perpetual peace. How can there be perpetual peace? Is it not that we mock ourselves?"

"I do not think so," Willoughby Johns declared. "There has never before been such a unanimous and vociferous European Press. This pact of ours, through its sheer simplicity, seems to have touched the imagination of millions."

The great ball at the American Embassy to celebrate the formal signing of the greatest of written documents since the Magna Charta was in full swing. The Marchese, however, felt that he had done his duty. A young Prince connected with the Royal House, whom he had been asked to look after, was safely established in the ballroom outside. He himself had kissed the fingers of his hostess and paid his devoirs to the Ambassador some time ago. He was forming one now of a *parti carré* with the Right Honourable Willoughby Johns, the English Premier, Prince von Fürstenheim, German Ambassador, and Monsieur Vallauris, the newly appointed delegate of his country from the Quai d'Orsay.

"I tell you what it is," the last-named remarked in an outburst half-cynical, half-humorous. "We ambassadors have cut our own throats. What I mean is this. There is no work to be done—no reason for our small army of secretaries and typists. Diplomacy will become a dead letter. Commerce! Commerce! Commerce! That is all our people, at any rate, think about. My visitors, my correspondents, all have to do with matters which concern our consular department."

"Capital!" Willoughby Johns commented. "I always thought that the two establishments—diplomatic and commercial—should be joined up."

"Nowadays," Von Fürstenheim pronounced, "there is as much diplomacy in dealing with the commerce of our country as was ever required in the settlement of weightier affairs."

"It is a new era upon which we enter," the Marchese declared.

"I ask myself and you," Vallauris propounded, "what is to be the reward which will be offered to this almost unknown person who first of all conceived the idea of the Pact and then carried it through?"

"Perhaps I can answer that question," Willoughby Johns observed, lighting a fresh cigarette. "It has been rather a trouble to all of us. What are you to do with a man who is himself a multi-millionaire, who cannot accept a title because he is an American and whose sole desire seems to be to step back into obscurity? However, between us—the Marchese and me—we have done all that is humanly possible. I, or rather my Cabinet, we have presented him with an island and the Marchese has given him a wife."

"An island?" Vallauris repeated, a trifle bewildered.

Willoughby Johns nodded assent.

"The island," he confided, "is the most beautiful one— although of course it is very small—ever owned by the

British Government, and the Princess Elida di Rezco di Vasena, the niece of our friend here, is, I think, quite one of the most beautiful of his country-people I have ever seen."

"An island," the Frenchman, who like most of his compatriots was of a social turn of mind, repeated incredulously. "Fancy wanting to live on an island!"

The Marchese smiled. There was a strange look in his eyes, for he, too, had known romance.

"You have never met my niece, Monsieur Vallauris," he observed.

EPILOGUE

THROUGH the driving grey mists of the Channel, battling her way against the mountainous seas of the Bay of Biscay, emerging at last into the rolling waters of the Straits and the sunshine of Gibraltar, the famous yacht *Espérance* seemed in a sense to be making one of those allegorical voyages of the Middle Ages dimly revealed in ancient volumes of fable and verse. Something of the same spirit had, perhaps, already descended upon her two passengers—Martin Fawley and Elida—as they passed into the warm tranquillity of the Mediterranean. After the turmoil of the last few months a sort of dreaming inertia seemed to have gathered them into her bosom. They were never tired of sitting in their favourite corner on deck, searching the changing sea by day and the starlit or cloud-bespattered sky by night, indulging in odd little bursts of spasmodic conversation, sometimes breaking a silence Elida, for her part declared, with the sole purpose of assuring herself that the whole affair was not a dream.

In the long daylight hours a new gaiety seemed to have come to her. She was restless with her happiness. She moved about the ship the very spirit of joy—light-footed, a miracle of grace and fantastic devotion to her very little more sedate lover. With the coming of night, however, her mood changed. She needed reassurance—Martin's arm and lips, the deep obscurity of their retired resting-place. There was excitement in the very throbbing of the engines. There were times when she felt herself shivering with the tremors of repressed passion. Martin surprised himself at the effortless facility with which, at such times, he played the part of lover and husband. With him, too, it seemed, after the hurricane of a stormy life, the opening of the great book of peace and romance....

It was seldom that they spoke of the immediate past. Both seemed equally convinced that it belonged to two utterly different people who would some day slowly awaken into life rubbing their eyes. Patches of those colourful days, however, would sometimes present themselves. One morning Elida discovered her husband with a powerful telescope watching the distant land. She paused by his side—a silent questioner.

"Somewhere amongst that nest of mountains," he pointed out with a grim smile of reminiscence, "is a French General—a fine little chap and I should think a thorough soldier—the desire of whose life it was to see me with a bandage over my eyes, against his white-washed barrack walls, facing a squad of his picked rifle-shots! Nearly came off, too!"

She shivered and half closed her eyes. He understood that she was shutting out Europe from the field of her vision. He closed the telescope with a little snap.

"We both had our escapes," he remarked. "Berati was out for your blood once.... It is my watch," he added, listening to the bell. "Come with me on the bridge for an hour."

She passed her arm through his and they mounted the steps together. The third officer made his report, saluted and withdrew. For several minutes afterwards no words passed. Fawley, leaning a little forward over the canvas-screened rail, scanned the horizon with seaman's vision. At such times a sort of graven calm came to his features, a new intensity to his keenly searching eyes. The blood of his sea-faring ancestors revealed itself. Deliberately, it seemed as though of natural habit, he examined with meticulous care every yard of the grey tossing waters. Only when he felt himself master of the situation did his features relax. He smiled down at Elida, drew her hand through his arm and commenced their nightly promenade.

Silence on the bridge. Sometimes he wondered whether they were not both grateful for that stern commandment of the sea. At ordinary times they were overwhelmed with the happiness which was always seeking to express itself. The silences of night were wonderful. The forced silences of the day were like an aching relief. A few paragraphs in a modern novel which she had passed to him with a smile contained sentences which struck home to them both.

"'The self-consciousness of the lover has increased enormously since the decay of Victorian sentimentalism. Allegorically speaking, it is only amongst the brainless and the lower orders of to-day that the man walks unashamed with his arm around his sweetheart's waist and both scorn to wait till the darkness for the mingling of lips. The affection of Edwin and Angelina of the modern world may be of the same order as that which inspired their great-grandmother and great-grandfather, but they seem to have lost the idea of how to set about it. In town this seems to be a fair idea of what goes on. Edwin and Angelina find themselves by accident alone.

"'What about a spot of love-making, old dear?' Edwin suggested apprehensively.

"'All right, old bean, but for heaven's sake don't let's moon about alone! We'll ring up Morris's Bar and see if any of the crowd are over there.'

"'Or if the amorous couple happen to be in the country, the reply to the same question is a feverish suggestion that they try if the old bus will do over sixty, or rival bags of golf clubs are produced, or Edwin is invited to search for his gun and come along and see if there's an odd rabbit sitting outside the woods....'"

Fawley closed the volume with a laugh.

"Let us be content to belong to the old-fashioned crowd," he suggested. "You come, anyhow, of a race which expresses itself far more naturally than we Anglo-Saxons can, and whether I am self-conscious about it or not I am not in the least ashamed of owning that I am absolutely and entirely in love with you."

She stretched out her arms.

"Come and tell me so again, darling," she invited. "Tell me so many times during the day. Do not let us care what any of these moderns are doing. Keep on telling me so."

Which invitation and his prompt acceptance of it seemed to form the textbook of their wonderful cruise.

And then at last their voyage came to an end. In the pearly grey stillness before the dawn they found themselves one morning on deck, leaning over the rail watching a dark mass ahead gradually take to itself definite shape. A lighthouse gave pale warning of a nearby harbour. The stars faded and a faint green light in the east broke into the coming day. They heard the ringing down of the engine behind. They were passing through the placid waters now at half-speed. The shape and colour of that dark mass gradually resolved themselves. The glimmering light sunk into obscurity. There were rolling woods and pine-topped hills surrounding the old-fashioned town of quaintly shaped buildings which they were slowly approaching. Behind there was a great sweep of meadowland—a broad ribbon of deep green turf—cut so many ages ago that it seemed as though it must have been a lordly avenue from all time. At the head was a dim vista of flower gardens surrounding the castle, from the turrets of which the streaming flag had already caught the morning breeze. One other building towered over the little town—the cathedral, half in ruins, half still massive and important. As they drew nearer they could hear the chimes, the sound of bells floating over the water. He pressed her arm.

"No salute," he warned her. "Someone told me there was not a gun upon the island."

"Is that not rather wonderful?" she whispered. "We have had all two people need of strife. The bells are better."

They were near enough now to hear the birds in the woods which hung over the low cliffs. A flight of duck surprised them. The chiming of the bells grew more melodious. There was a little catch in her voice as her arms reached out for him.

"The people on the quay may see us, but I do not care," she whispered. "This is Paradise which we have found."

THE END